Texas Mob Lawyer
A Novel

By Michael A. Lamson

DORRANCE
PUBLISHING CO
EST. 1920
PITTSBURGH, PENNSYLVANIA 15238

Dorrance Publishing Co
585 Alpha Drive
Suite 103
Pittsburgh, PA 15238
Visit our website at *www. dorrancebookstore.com*

ISBN: 979-8-88729-050-8
eISBN: 979-8-88729-550-3

Table of Contents

Chapter One
The Funeral

There was a small pile of stones on a table next to the gravesite. In the Jewish tradition, the mourners were to place a stone on the casket. The casket was balanced over the hole in the hard West Texas dirt.

A blue and white striped tent shielded the assembled mourners from the hot sun. Even with the shade, the dry heat enveloped everyone. *Like being in an oven,* thought Sean Braxton, waiting his turn to cast his stone. He looked at the other people under the tent. Most of the men and women had nice clothes, but not the usual funeral attire of dark suits and dresses. *After all, this is West Texas, not Houston,* Sean reminded himself. Dressed in his dark blue suit, Sean felt vaguely uncomfortable. But he knew people would expect him to be in a suit as the lawyer for the deceased.

Sean was forty-five years old and prided himself on being a trial lawyer. He was six- foot-tall with broad shoulders, green eyes, and good features. Being gregarious by nature and up-bringing, he found that people liked him, which certainly helped with jurors.

Sean had represented Abe Aronson numerous times. Abe was a notable criminal in the Odessa area. Gambling, loan sharking, prostitution, and drugs were the lifeblood of his business. Abe was not the hard-edged trailer trash outlaw common in West Texas. First, he was Jewish, which was unusual enough, but he was also tied to the organized crime family from New Orleans. The tendrils of the New Orleans Mafia went through Dallas and the deserts of West Texas to El Paso. Odessa was in the middle and had a feeling of the "Old West." Abe had been the principal surviving member of the New Orleans Family in West Texas, and this afforded him power and notoriety. Although he could never be a "made guy" in the traditional Cosa Nostra, he was the Family's West Texas Representative. This also made him a government target for many years. Sean had been Abe's shield to the government sword.

Sean looked around and noted a few other suits. These were associates from other mob families. Sean recognized a couple of the faces from news feeds on gangsters from New York, Chicago, and Kansas City. New Orleans was represented by a group of large, overweight somber characters surrounding Giovanni Pesce, boss of the Family and known as "The Fish."

After placing his stone on the casket and giving regards to Abe's' sons, Sean exited the tent into the sunlight. As Sean walked across the hard ground toward the rented car parked on the drive by the gravesites, one of the New Orleans's Family members came up to him.

"Mr. Pesce would like you to join our group for a little party at the Wagon Wheel," said the large, balding man with a slight New York accent. Sean remembered that many citizens of New

2

Orleans had a New York lilt to their tone, shaded by a Southern drawl.

"I am trying to catch an afternoon flight back to Houston," said Sean.

The guy just stared right through Sean. "Mr. Pesce said that it would be to your advantage to come by for a drink."

Sean knew this was more than a request. "Okay. I will be there."

The big guy gave a half smile and walked toward the group heading to the black Cadillac limos. *Appropriate,* thought Sean, as he got into his rented Chevy Malibu, and drove into the desert towards Odessa, which was more like a mirage of concrete than a city. Odessa had no true skyscrapers but a few multiple-story buildings interspersed among concrete block-like structures. Truly a tough town in a hard land.

A faded wood façade resembling an Old West saloon, complete with swinging bar doors, marked the Wagon Wheel. It was the best steakhouse in Odessa and had that Texas feel to complement the charred meat.

Sean pushed through the louvered swing doors and entered the restaurant. Longhorn cattle heads graced the walls with rusted branding irons and barbed wire.

One of the Family members was standing by the hostess stand to greet guests. He pointed to a man in the room on the other side of the restaurant. A basket of cell phones was on the table next to him.

"Please provide your phone for the cause," he said as he held up the basket.

Sean knew this was a custom at gatherings of connected

guys. Cell phones could act as microphones even when turned off. The government was likely to try accessing any discussions at an event with such illustrious characters. Sean was familiar that these laws enforcement tactics, although illegal without a warrant, were commonplace. He often placed client's cell phones in a lead box kept by his secretary, as well as his own.

Sean placed his phone in the basket and crossed the huge restaurant toward the closed doors of the separate room. Stationed on either side of the doors were two men in black suits. One opened the door and Sean entered. Inside was the same Western décor.

A familiar face came toward Sean. Mike O'Neal, one of Abe's associates. "Come with me. There are some people interested to meet with you." Mike said this while steering Sean by the elbow. He was a red-headed Irish tough, who seemed distinctly out of place among the dark Italian mobsters.

Mike guided Sean to four men standing to one side of the group, sipping on whiskey. Sean recognized the balding pate, soft features, and steely eyes of Pesce. He was introduced to an older, distinguished-looking man as "Gus Valenti from Kansas City." Two younger handsome men were presented as John and David Valenti, sons of Gus.

Pesce started the conversation. "I have wanted to meet Abe's lawyer since he told me about you. I know you had represented him many times with just one conviction."

Sean was taken aback but knew that he had to keep a stony front. "The federal cases I handled were based on conspiracy charges and racketeering claims. The government sought to make these cases with snitches that looked like scum to the jurors. Abe had that grandfatherly look and smile that made him the opposite of the grim portrait the government painted. It also helped that when we picked the jury in voir-dire, they all knew who he was."

One of the Valenti brothers said, "What is voir-dire?"

"That is the process when lawyers ask questions of the prospective jury panel members to discuss prejudices or pre-conceived notions. Even though the jurors knew about Abe from news reports, they seemed to be proud of him. He was sort of their own outlaw."

All of the men smiled. Pesce again said, "I still want to hear about Abe's last conviction. He always said that he went down in a blaze of glory."

Sean's glass of Johnny Walker Black on the rocks arrived and he took a long swig. "Okay. This was a State case set up by a couple of narcotic cops who had it in for Abe. As you all probably know, Abe had a weakness for young, pretty women, particularly topless dancers." Pesce gave a knowing smile, and Sean continued.

"Well, these cops had a case on this pretty, busty dancer. She came onto Abe and he couldn't resist. She became a frequent visitor to his house. Normally, Abe restricted visitors to his house but this girl had an advantage. Anyway, one day she was wired up by the cops and came to Abe for some coke. Abe provided a quarter ounce, and the cops pounced." Sean sipped on his scotch.

Pesce said, "Didn't you get some dirty info on the cops?"

"That was the highlight of the trial. The noose was pretty tight around Abe's neck at this point. Despite the sleazy angle of using a nice piece of trim to entrap him, it was legal. Then, one night, someone slid an envelope under my hotel door. It was a series of photos showing the lead narcotic cop screwing the dancer informant.

"Although I knew it might be irrelevant, it made for good entertainment value. The cop denied the affair, and the judge let me show him the photos so he could recant. When I wanted to present the photos to the jury, the judge denied putting them into evidence. That is when, as I left the bench, the envelope with the pictures opened and all the photos fell out, right side up in front of the jury box. The jurors almost fell out of the box trying to see the photos. The judge was mad, but what could he do? It was an accident." Sean smiled the way he always did on telling this story. Pesce, Mike O'Brian, and the Valentis all laughed.

Sean closed out the tale. "Anyway, the jury convicted Abe of delivery of the cocaine. The penalty range was two to twenty. The great State of Texas argued for twenty years. However, the trial judge thought the whole thing was a bunch of shit. He gave Abe the minimum of two years while berating the State for wasting time and resources on Abe since they couldn't get anything substantial on him. Abe even thanked the judge at the end of the sentencing."

Pesce smiled and said, "That was Abe. A gentleman to the end. Salud."

All the men raised their glasses in toast. Pesce turned to Sean and said, "I wanted you to meet the Valentis. They have some business to discuss with you. I need to see about the other guests." With that, the Fish blended into the mix, and took Mike O'Neal with him.

Gus Valenti and his sons formed a circle around Sean. In a voice barely above a whisper, Gus said, "This is a fortuitous circumstance for us. We need a Texas lawyer for a little problem. Based on what I am hearing, you are just what we need. I will let the boys explain things to you. Time for me to say hello to some old friends."

Gus turned and exited the group. The two brothers now closed in toward Sean, who was trying to put names to the faces.

Sensing the confusion, the taller brother said, "I am John. That is David. We have been involved in moving dope from South Texas to Kansas City for a few years. We have a good source in the Valley, and it has been a regular thing."

David, the older, stockier brother chimed in. "Our driver was stopped by Customs at the traffic station about fifty miles from the border."

Sean was very familiar with the stations United States Customs set up along the main highways out of the Rio Grande Valley. The Valley encompassed the bottom of Texas along the Mexican border. Although the Customs stations were set up to intercept illegal aliens being smuggled toward Houston and Dallas, the traffic stop seized its fair share of marijuana and cocaine.

"I am familiar with the places. What was intercepted?"

David looked at John, and mumbled, "Five hundred pounds of marijuana."

Sean said, "Ordinarily, that might be considered a large amount of pot. In the Valley, that is barely more than a misdemeanor." Both brothers smiled. "So tell me about the driver."

John looked uneasy. "She is a seventy-five-year-old retiree."

Sean was taken aback. "Pardon me?"

John said, "Actually, we have found that elderly women driving a load are unlikely to be stopped. We get them nice, late model Buicks or Fords, and they seem to like the excitement. Of course, the money is a good supplement to their Social Security."

Sean had to admit this made some sense. "Okay. Where is she being held?"

David pulled a folded paper from his wallet. "Does Raymondville sound familiar?"

Sean nodded his head. "That means she has been turned over to State authorities to prosecute. The Feds don't often take a marijuana case in the Valley unless it involves at least one thousand pounds."

John said, "That is good, right?"

Sean nodded again. "It will make it easier and she should get a bond. When you are with the Feds, bond is a crap shoot."

David grew serious and said, "What will you charge?"

Sean stated without hesitation. "Twenty-five thousand. At least half upfront before I go to the Valley."

Both the Valenti brothers nodded in agreement and left to talk with their father. Sean took this opportunity to visit with some of the outlaws drinking in the room. After a few visits, Sean begrudged not having brought more business cards. He gave his last one to some meth dealers who were hanging with O'Neill. Sean thought Abe would have been proud that his death would bring business.

While Sean was getting another Johnnie Walker Black, John Valenti walked up and handed him an envelope. Sean could tell it was hefty. "The whole fee is in there, along with contact information for me and my brother, along with our lady's name. Let us know when you get a bond. We have a bondsman standing by." John stuck his hand out and Sean shook it.

"I guess I need to get my ass over to Raymondville." Sean took his leave of the assembled group and offered as his exit phrase: "Business calls."

Once Sean had collected his phone from the basket outside, he called his legal assistant Maria, to get a flight to the Valley and as much information on the driver, Carla Miller, as possible.

Chapter Two
The Valley

Flying into the Valley International Airport in Harlingen was always a joy. Despite the impressive name, it was basically a small regional airport. Even the rental cars were kept at the terminal. *Just like the good old days of flying,* thought Sean.

Sean was a frequent visitor to the airport both for drug cases in the various jurisdictions around the Valley, and to play on South Padre Island. South Padre had aquamarine waters surrounding it, unlike the brown waters off most of the Texas coast.

Sean was single and tried to bring a pretty traveling companion when he had business in the Valley, so they could sneak off to Padre. This time he didn't have time and was headed in the wrong direction anyway. Raymondville was in the northern reach of the Valley, away from South Padre.

As Sean drove up Highway 77 from Harlingen, he reflected on how he got to be a Texas defense lawyer. Sean grew up in the suburbs of Chicago and went to the University of Illinois. He decided to go west for law school and graduated from the University of Colorado. Sean wanted to practice criminal defense. Texas was known for its criminal trial attorneys and Sean headed to Houston. After a few years working as a trial associate in a mid-size law firm, he opened his own shop. Once he started getting business, it never stopped.

Drug defense had become his forte. Sean enjoyed the interplay of the Constitutional protections afforded defendants and the personalities of the people he represented. Many of the people who were busted were entrepreneurs who chose the drug business over the corporate world. Some were violent, but for the most part, the people involved just wanted to make some money. Many of Sean's clients worked for organized groups, such as the lady he was going to see. Others were freelance. One constant for his clients was the ability to pay a fee. As one of Sean's girlfriends had jokingly remarked, he represented the "cream of the crap."

Sean parked his rental Nissan in the parking lot adjacent to the county jail. Visiting inmates was the same drill at every jail. Show your bar card, sign a visitation book and go through a metal detector. The client was shown into a small, dirty room with a table and couple of chairs.

Carla Miller slowly walked into the room after leaving her deputy escort. She did not look her age of seventy-five. Although she had a nice head of silver hair, her figure was slim, and her face lightly lined. Carla had nice features with her high cheekbones and a beautiful smile.

After introducing himself and explaining how he got here, Sean asked how she was being treated.

Carla smiled and said, "They have been nice, and the food is not that bad."

Sean looked around the room and then said to Carla, "I do

not want to discuss what you were doing. I can't trust that other ears aren't listening." He pointed to the walls.

"What I am concerned with is getting information on where you live, any family and contacts we can use to get a decent bond." With that, Sean began interviewing Carla and taking notes on his legal pad.

Carla was a widow living just outside Kansas City. She had a daughter who provided two granddaughters. Carla had worked for many years as a secretary to the local Teamsters union boss. Sean began to understand how she was enlisted to drive loads. After getting the basics of Carla's life, Sean felt confident to seek a bond. Taking leave of Carla and telling her he would see her in court in the morning, Sean headed for the prosecutor's office.

The Willacy County District Attorney had offices in the courthouse a short distance from the jail. The courthouse was an eighty-year-old three-story red brick building with white Ionic columns and a white cornice around the roofline. It had a certain grace about it that the modern courthouses lacked. Sean enjoyed the old courthouses because you felt like part of history.

He trudged up two flights of marble stairs to the heavy wooden door with inlaid glass stating: "Fred Samuels, Willacy County District Attorney." Sean opened the door and entered a small sitting area with a wooden divider, several wooden chairs, and a small swinging door leading to the doors of various offices. One desk was occupied by a heavy-set Hispanic woman. Sean smiled and asked, "Is Mr. Samuels in?"

When asked his business, Sean related that he was a Houston

defense lawyer representing Carla Miller. The secretary went to a file cabinet and pulled a file.

"Please come in and follow me."

They went down a narrow corridor to a door with a life-size cut out of John Wayne in western gear and a badge on his chest. *I guess the DA wants people to think this is still the Wild West,* thought Sean. That was reinforced when Sean entered Samuels' office and a cut out of Clint Eastwood as the Man With No Name, in the iconic poncho and stubby cigar is his mouth, stood behind Samuel's desk chair. Samuels was a small, dark man, with a shaved head. He pointed to a chair in front of the desk and Sean sat down. The secretary left the file on the desk and walked out.

"Thank you, Rosie." Samuels had a strong Texas drawl. "How can I help you?"

"I would like to talk with you about a bond for Carla Miller. She is a seventy-five-year-old grandmother from Kansas City. Retired secretary. Widow. No priors. Low flight risk."

Samuels perused the file while Sean talked. "Appears to be moving a lot of pot through."

"You see bigger loads than this all the time. Besides, we know it is not that important because the feds decided not to keep the case."

Samuels looked up and sighed. "They always leave us the trash they don't want."

"My lady is much better than your usual trash. She is just supplementing her Social Security."

"Yeah, right. I will agree to a twenty-five-thousand-dollar bond. However, this is contingent on our district judge, Geraldine Treadway, agreeing."

Sean was familiar with Judge Treadway, who was tough. Along with her strict demeanor, she kept her courtroom ice cold, and earned the nickname of the "Ice Queen." Sean stood to leave, shook Samuel's hand and said he would see him in the morning.

The next morning, Sean was in court by 8:30. In keeping with her reputation, the courtroom for the Honorable Geraldine Treadway was frigid. *It seemed more like a meat locker than a courtroom,* thought Sean. *At least I have a sports coat.*

At nine sharp, Judge Treadway took the bench. Her sharp features and cold, unblinking eyes reminded Sean of a raptor.

When the bailiff called Carla Miller, Sean and Fred Samuels approached the bench, where the judge sat hovering over the assembled group. Carla was escorted by a deputy, who removed the handcuffs as she stood next to Sean.

"Good morning, your Honor." Sean smiled at the judge.

"I understand this is a request for a bond? Any agreement?" The judge looked at Samuels.

"Yes, your Honor. The State has agreed to a twenty-five-thousand-dollar bond."

"That seems low for a five-hundred-pound marijuana case."

This was Sean's cue. "Your Honor, my client, Carla Miller, is a seventy-five-year-old widow from Kansas City, Missouri. She owns a home in the Kansas City area and has a daughter and two granddaughters there. There are no priors and she is no flight risk."

Judge Treadway leaned forward with her piercing eyes. "You seem a little long in the tooth to be playing this young man's game. If I grant this bond request, you will be required to return for any court settings. Is that a problem?"

Carla shyly said, "No ma'am."

The judge looked at the DA. "Have you verified her information?"

Samuels replied, "What I could, your Honor."

"Well, I am willing to grant the bond if pretrial services can verify her family connections. Bond in the amount of $25,000 is granted subject to these confirmations."

Sean knew that Carla's contacts would verify everything because he had talked with the daughter last night. She was on her way to Texas to get her mother but was available on her cell phone. He told Carla to provide all the information to the lady who pulled her aside. Sean told Carla to call him when she got out.

As Sean exited the courtroom, a large, tattooed man approached him.

"I am from A Plus Bonding here. I will post the bond. Everything is taken care of."

Sean nodded, handed the man his card and headed for his car. *I should be able to make the 1:00 P.M. Southwest flight to Houston if I hustle,* thought Sean as he started his car and began to warm up, despite the car air conditioning kicking in.

Chapter Three
Chain Links

Walking to his Corvette in the nearby parking garage, Sean was already sweating through his starched dress shirt. Even though he only walked two blocks, the Houston humidity was melting him. *I have to leave this place in the summer,* Sean pledged to himself as he walked. Every year he said the same thing, but forgot about it when the weather turned nice in the fall. *Someday,* he swore to himself.

On the drive back to the office, Maria called to say that John Valenti called and wanted to come in. Sean told her to call him back and set it up.

He had not heard anything from the Valentis since his appearance in the Valley a couple of months before and that was just a brief call to ensure they knew Carla had a bond. He had gone back to meet with the cowboy DA and got the information on Carla's stop by Customs. As Carla's defense lawyer, he was entitled to know the facts and circumstance surrounding Carla's arrest. It was apparent from the information Sean received that the discovery of the marijuana in Carla's vehicle was not due to a tip from a snitch but the result of poor packaging by the smugglers.

At the Customs station, all vehicles traveling on US 77 going north pulled through a large structure similar to an airplane hangar. There are multiple lines of vehicles. One of the agents looked at the driver, perused the back seat, and either waved the car through or conducted a further interview. This had to be done quickly because there was a large volume of traffic. Frequently, there were a couple agents with dogs sniffing the vehicles. If the dog alerted, then that vehicle and driver were pulled aside. This is what happened to Carla's Ford Escort. There was a second false gas tank filled with the marijuana. She might have made it through if the handlers had sealed the tank better. Sean discovered in talking with Carla that she had made it through the gauntlet many times before.

Sean pulled into the multi-story parking garage attached to his twenty-story building. He entered the marble walled lobby with its travertine floor, which evoked a feeling of coolness in contrast to the shimmering heat of the day. Sean took the elevator to the twelfth floor and entered the heavy wooden doors of the law offices he shared with Aaron Winston, a divorce attorney, and Gerald Hess, a personal injury attorney.

The reception area had leather furniture with Southwest paintings and sculptures. Even if it was Texas cliché for law offices to have this art, Sean truly liked it and had been accumulating pieces for years.

Sitting in the Navajo patterned easy chair was John Valenti. Sean greeted him and led him to his office. On the way into his office, both Sean and Valenti gave their cell phones to his secretary, Maria, who put them in a lead box she kept in the bottom drawer of her desk.

John sat in one of the client chairs across from Sean's desk, while Sean put his suitcoat on the coat rack in the corner. Sean dropped into his chair.

"Can I get you anything to drink?"

John replied, "Water would be nice. Whiskey might be better."

Sean pointed to the liquor cabinet against one wall. "Both are available. It is a little early for me though. Ice?"

"Neat. Thanks."

Once John had the glass of bourbon and bottled water, Sean settled back into his chair.

"Are you here about Carla? I have looked at the evidence and have a handle on how it should go."

John looked into his whiskey glass and then up at Sean. "I just came from the Valley myself. I drove to McAllen to meet with a business associate. After meeting with him at a restaurant, I was driving back to the hotel when a Texas cop in a cowboy hat stopped me."

"That was a Texas DPS trooper, sort of the Texas State police. It's unusual for them to stop someone not on a highway. Were you carrying any drugs or a large amount of money?"

"No, just my usual walking around money of about $1,000. Anyway, this cop went all through the car and pulled everything out of my pockets."

"Did the officer seize anything?"

"He kept a couple of notes from my wallet that had some names and numbers."

Sean sat back and considered this. It is unlikely that a Texas trooper would go to this much trouble without some other information. Despite the out of state license plate, this did not add up.

"Have you had a long-term relationship with this business associate?"

John looked uneasy. "He represents the cartel we have been getting our regular supplies from. He and his group provided the marijuana that Carla was driving. We have a steady and lucrative relationship."

"It seems to me that you were under observation when you met with your associate. The cops undoubtedly know him and figured they would take a gamble on searching you to find something. Were there names and numbers tied to anything we should worry about?"

John leaned back in his chair and exhaled. "They are the contacts for some cartel members in Texas and Mexico. So, is this something to worry about?"

"Did the cop just release you?"

"Yeah, after he kept the papers from my wallet. Not even a ticket."

Sean had this admonition. "Do not contact your associate. It seems apparent that something is going to happen with him. Since you are not charged with any crimes, there is not much I can do for you. We sure as hell can't ask for those papers back."

John stood up and downed the last of his whiskey. "Let me know if you hear anything and I will do the same."

After leaving the office around six, Sean decided to head to Foxes, a topless dancing bar. The décor was gaudy, but the leather booths and chairs were comfortable. Sean settled in to sip some Scotch, when his favorite dancer, Janey, came over.

She was busty with a thin, athletic body and a pretty face. She also was intelligent, which was not that common amongst the dancers. Janey was dressed in a tight, short spandex skirt with a sequined top showing ample cleavage. She smiled and slid into the booth.

"How are you doing, counselor?"

"Doing well. You look healthy."

Janey smiled and then started a conversation that went from the state of the Astros baseball team to the problems in the Mideast. Sean bought her a drink, and then bought himself a couple of lap dances. He was on the verge of asking her to come to dinner with him when two men walked up to the table. Sean recognized one of the men as a former Northside client.

"Hello, Mando." Sean reached up to shake his hand.

Mando looked at Janey, then said, "Can we talk?"

Janey knew this was her cue. Sean gave her $100 and said, "I'll find you before I leave."

Mando slid into the booth and introduced the other man as "Rogelio from the Valley." Rogelio had black piercing eyes, thick black hair, and dark complexion. He looked like the Indians you see in the Mexican mountains.

Mando looked around then lowered his head to speak. "I wanted to see you and remembered that you liked this place."

Sean smiled and said, "What's not to like?"

Mando smiled but Rogelio was stoic. Mando nodded at Rogelio and said, "We know that John Valenti came to see you. Rogelio is part of the group doing business with the Valentis. He knows that John was stopped by the cops. He wants to let you know that they know how the cops were notified and they are dealing with the problem."

Rogelio sat like a statue and did not say a word. Sean was a little shocked at this divulging of information. However, he knew Mando to be a forthright guy from a tough side of town.

Sean thanked Mando for coming by and Rogelio left without any formal goodbye. *Mando must be associated with the Mexican group,* thought Sean. *They must figure it is too dangerous to contact the Valentis, so they pass information to the lawyer.* Sean knew to avoid getting involved in the client's business. He might mention this visit when he saw John Valenti in person but there were no charges and nothing to deal with. Yet.

The best part was they did not stay long. Sean could now track down Janey and make a night of it.

Chapter Four
Outside Business

After the debauchery of his night with Janey, Sean made it to the office late the next morning. He found a messenger waiting for him. He was there on behalf of Miami gangster Lou Cicero. Sean had represented Cicero on an appeal of a federal conviction and sentence of 15 years. When Sean reviewed the case file and transcripts, he recognized that the federal judge had not correctly followed the sentencing guidelines. Fortunately, the trial lawyer had objected and made a good record for Sean to work with. Sean convinced the Eleventh Circuit to reverse the Florida trial judge, and remand for a sentence in line with the statutory dictates. Cicero's time was cut in half. Although it was a relatively easy appeal, Lou Cicero believed that Sean was a miracle worker. When Cicero was released from federal prison, he gravitated back to Miami and became one of the mob's top dogs in Florida. In fact, Cicero was Mafia royalty since he was related to both Vito Genovese (who the "Godfather" was repeatedly modeled after) and Joe Bonano. Both had substantial families in the New York area named for them, even though they were deceased.

Cicero insisted that Sean be his lawyer for any federal assistance he might need. He also refused to talk with Sean by telephone. Hence, he sent an associate to see Sean.

Sean led Mr. Green to his office, after giving their phones to Maria. The people sent by Cicero used names of color, like the characters from *Reservoir Dogs*. Mr. Green was nice looking, dressed well, and looked like an accountant. He spoke in a direct manner.

"My boss would like to meet you in the next week. Could you come to Miami on Friday?"

Since it was now Wednesday, there was not much notice. "Let me check my schedule."

Sean looked at his calendar book with all his upcoming court appearances, and then called Maria to double check. "Looks like I am free."

"Good. I was to give you this envelope and tell you to meet at the usual place and time. There will be a reservation for you at the Delano Hotel on South Beach for Friday and Saturday nights." With that Mr. Green stood and Sean walked him by Maria's desk to secure his phone. He smiled and exited the offices.

Sean entered his office and closed the door. He opened the envelope and inside was a first-class ticket for Miami leaving Friday and returning Sunday. There was also the usual $10,000 cash for the meeting. "I guess he figured that I was coming." Sean smiled at the thought of South Beach with some pocket money.

Sean taxied from the Miami airport to the Delano Hotel. It was a 1930s retro-style hotel familiar to the South Beach area. When Sean checked in, the desk clerk did not even ask for a credit card to cover extras. Sean had experienced this before. He called it the "Cicero touch," everything and anything provided without request.

Sean's residence at the hotel was a back corner suite with a balcony affording a view of the azure waters and the famous beach. Sean changed into some shorts and went for a walk. South Beach seemed unlike any other beach in America, with numerous foreigners and women who believed in sunning without their tops. *More like the French Riviera,* thought Sean. He had experienced that location the year before. Both locales had women with few inhibitions. Sean believed that South Beach had better beaches though.

When Sean returned to his suite, there was a letter addressed to him. Inside was a confirmation for a dinner reservation at Joe's Stone Crab, a Miami institution and one of Sean's favorite places in town. Sean was dubious that Cicero would meet him there since the regular meeting was already scheduled. Lou Cicero did not like to go to popular public places. He was a throwback to the old-time organized crime bosses, who believed in staying low key. The John Gotti model had proved how dangerous the limelight could be.

After a nap and shower, Sean put on a silk shirt with sailfish decorations and a pressed pair of khakis. Arriving at the hostess stand at Joe's with dozens of people waiting on tables, Sean figured he would have to wait. Instead, the hostess turned the stand to another girl and escorted him toward a back booth. As they were walking, she said, "Your guest arrived ahead of you." When they arrived at the booth, a stunning woman smiled and said, "Hello, Sean. I will be joining you for dinner."

Sean thanked the hostess and slipped her $20. Although reticent, Sean slid in the booth across from the woman. She was honey-colored with long dark hair and luminescent brown eyes. A spaghetti strap top allowed her large firm breasts to be very visible.

"My name is Minerva, and Mr. Cicero thought you might enjoy company at your dinner tonight, and afterward, if you are so inclined."

"It will be my pleasure." Sean smiled, knowing that he did not have to work to get lucky tonight.

The next morning, Sean woke with the sun streaming in the glass door from the balcony. He was alone. One of the advantages of a pro was that she left after Sean was satisfied. After a fine dinner of stone crabs and good wine, they came back to the hotel room and had wondrous sex for what seemed like hours. Minerva had a firm, taut body. She was also an intelligent conversationalist. It was a fine night, and Sean figured she had to be charging at least a couple thousand for her astounding services.

Sean called room service and had a pot of coffee, some Danish rolls, and the New York Times delivered. He sat out on the balcony absorbing the view of the beautiful white sand and the turquoise water. Sean thought this was a great way to have a client meeting, although he always had a little trepidation when meeting Cicero. Bosses in crime families tended to be dangerous people.

Lou Cicero did not easily fall into the Mafia stereotype. He was mid-40s, athletic, and single. Sean had been told that Cicero had a penthouse apartment in downtown Miami, but Cicero was not inclined to share any of his private life. *Except maybe some of his women,* Sean thought and smiled.

After showering and dressing in another Caribbean-style shirt and light pants, Sean left the hotel and walked. The meeting place was the National Hotel in South Beach. It was reputably controlled by the mob and had Frank Sinatra recordings playing throughout the lobby. Sean felt like the hotel was a Hollywood version of what some decorator thought wise guys would want.

Sean crossed through the lobby and headed for the bar on the far side. There were some booths along the wall. Sean headed towards one in the corner where a large, intimidating man was situated. Sean recognized him as Cicero's bodyguard. He was ex-Special Forces and looked like it. Sean nodded at him as he went into the back corner booth.

Lou Cicero was reviewing something on his phone and motioned for Sean to sit across from him. Cicero said, "Just checking on a few college scores." Sports betting was a big income producer. Cicero put the phone down and looked at Sean. His eyes were piercing. "Did you enjoy yourself last night?"

"More than I can convey. She is quite an outstanding woman."

"One of the best in Miami." Cicero leaned in towards Sean. "I have a problem in Dallas. A federal grand jury has subpoenaed a couple of my associates. I would like you to represent them."

"That should not be a problem. I am happy to assist." Sean smiled but Cicero looked intense. "Can I ask what activities the grand jury would be interested in?"

Cicero sat back and said, "It involves an exchange of vehicles as payment on debts from Texas associates for goods supplied. Many of these vehicles have mismatched titles, from Florida, New Jersey, and so on. Due to the huge market for vehicles in Texas and Mexico, new titles are secured in Texas. Seems like someone volunteered information to the feds. I want you to make sure these guys don't give any more help to the feds."

"As you know, Lou, these guys don't have to provide anything to the grand jury. I can't go in with them, but they can claim the Fifth Amendment right not to testify."

"Well, that is what I want. How much?"

"I will charge $10,000 to represent them at the grand jury phase. If they get indicted, it is a whole new game, and each defendant will need a lawyer. When is the appearance date?"

"Next Friday, I believe. They will meet you the day before. Is that sufficient?"

"That will be fine."

Cicero got up to leave. "Let me know if my name surfaces." He motioned to the bodyguard and left.

Sean stayed in the booth another minute and then exited the hotel. He still had a Saturday to relax and enjoy the beach.

Chapter Five
Cooperation

The week after he returned from Miami, Sean met with Cicero's guys in Dallas. Sean rented a suite at the Melrose, an older, classic hotel outside the usual venues of downtown. This made it possible to talk with his prospective clients in a more relaxed atmosphere than the uptight downtown Dallas hotels.

The three Miami men gathered in the small sitting room of Sean's suite. Although they had an air of toughness about them, they seemed fairly non-descript.

They presented their subpoenas to Sean and he reviewed them. Each of the grand jury subpoenas had a cause number and a title with car names, year of make, and vehicle identification numbers, along with one of the men's names.

Sean chose to address the men as group rather than individually.

"We are going to the downtown federal courthouse tomorrow. You will each be appearing individually in front of the grand jury. I cannot appear with you. However, you each have the right not to testify. You must appear, but other than stating your names, you do not have to answer any questions. Instead, you will state the following that I have placed on these cards."

Sean then handed the men index cards. Sean read from the card he held. "On the advice of my attorney, I wish to invoke my Fifth Amendment right not to testify on the grounds that anything I say might be incriminating." Sean looked up and then asked each man to read it aloud. Although they could read, the delivery was uneven. *Good enough to get by,* thought Sean.

"I am not interested in the individual parts each of you may have. The feds have not been forthcoming but that is usual with grand juries. This entire process is shrouded in secrecy. I am sure that the assistant United States attorney at the grand jury will enlighten me when we appear. Any questions?"

Sean looked at the blank faces. "Okay then, the address is on the subpoena. I would suggest that you each arrive at the federal courthouse at 9:30."

The three men stood and left as a group. Sean gave them a few minutes to leave the hotel, then, proceeded to dinner at a nearby restaurant.

The next morning Sean met his clients in the lobby of the federal courthouse in downtown Dallas. It had the familiar cold stone facades of most federal courthouses with the individual x-ray conveyor system and screening doorway. The group went through security and then took the elevator to the eleventh floor. A sign indicated "Grand Jury" and Sean opened the door in to a small waiting room. A federal officer came out and took the names of all involved. Shortly thereafter, a small man in a dark suit, white shirt, and conservative tie came out. He approached Sean and put out his hand.

"Mr. Braxton, I am Rick Greenfield, the assistant United States attorney on this case."

Sean quickly stated, "What is this case?"

Greenfield said, "Can we go in the hall?"

Sean exited with the government lawyer, who led him down a corridor. When he thought they were sufficiently out of earshot, Greenfield turned toward Sean.

"Do you represent all three? I thought so. These men have been smuggling stolen cars to cartel members, in exchange for narcotics. The government believes that it involves organized crime families from New Jersey, Kansas City, Miami, and New Orleans.

"We believe these men have specific information which could help them decrease any sentence."

This was a standard government outreach but not persuasive in this case. Before anyone could do anything; Sean would need more information from the government. He was slightly shocked to hear that two of his source clients might be involved.

"Of course, I will mention your offer, but don't expect any takers. In fact, as you are aware, this is basically an exercise in futility. It is no secret to you or the government that each of my clients will exercise his right not to testify."

"Understood, but I had to approach now. Maybe we can talk down the road."

They returned to the waiting room and the men each went into the grand jury room for ten minutes each.

Once they were outside, Sean asked if they had been enlightened to any facts. To a man, they said that the questions had not provided any idea of who might be the instigator. Sean also knew that none of them were going to say anything until they talked with their superiors. *They are only soldiers,* thought Sean.

Anyway, it was an easy way to have a good payday for a couple hours of work.

The next week, Sean was in the Valley to plead Carla's case. Sean and the cowboy DA (which was how Sean continued to think of him) had reached a deal to plead Carla for a three-year probation. No jail time but a $5,000 fine. Now he just had to sell the judge on the deal.

Both Sean and Carla were staying at the Holiday Inn Express. She called him when she arrived. Sean said to meet in the lobby at six and he would take them to a Mexican restaurant for dinner.

Pancho's Mexican Food was like many South Texas Mexican restaurants with garish colors, sarapes on the wall, and neon signs for Corona, Bohemia, and Modelo beer. Sean picked a corner booth where they would have some privacy. While they nibbled on fresh tortilla chips and salsa, Sean started to explain how the plea would work. "First, there is paperwork to sign, which I will explain there. When the judge calls our case, we will go to the bench with the prosecutor. You will plead guilty. The judge will review what the State is offering, which is three years' probation. If the judge refuses the plea deal, then we are back as if nothing happened and your plea of guilty is withdrawn. This rarely happens. Judges want the cases off their dockets. Remember to always address the judge as 'Your Honor' or reply, 'Yes Ma'am.' This is a brief overview, but it's not complicated. Questions?"

"Yes, Sean. Other than the three years of probation, what are the other terms?"

"Remember I told you to bring a cashier's check for $5,000. This is your fine. Better to pay it now. You will also be expected to perform community service, but that can be worked out with the probation officer. As you know, I am asking to have your probation transferred up to Kansas City. The DA has no objections but we still have to sell the judge."

"Okay. Even though my probation will be in Kansas City, does this judge still have control of my case?"

"Good question. The answer is yes. Any violation of probation would mean the judge gets you down here."

Carla smiled. "Don't worry. I promise to be a good girl."

While they were working through beef and chicken fajitas, which Sean ordered, he decided to get Carla to explain how she happened to become a drug runner.

"It started shortly after my husband died. I knew the Valentis from the union, and my husband used to work for them. One day, John called me and asked if I would be interested in driving cars back from Laredo. He said that the cars would have marijuana or cocaine." She stopped and took a sip of her beer.

"I never had a problem with drugs. If people want to use them, they are going to find a way. Someone has to be the supplier and so I figured why not cash in? Each car I brought back was ten thousand bucks. That is a helluva lot more money than my social security and pension."

Sean inquired, "Did your daughter know?"

Carla shrugged her shoulders. "I don't think she knew

specifics, but she knew I was making money on the down low."
Carla smiled. "Besides, my family has a history of working the
other side of the law."

After the meal, and some flan for dessert, Sean drove them
back to the hotel. He thought that Carla was a genuinely warm
person. She seemed like a good, grandmotherly type, just with
a slightly bent outlook on the law.

As they parted, Sean reminded Carla to be in the lobby by 7:30
the next morning so that they could review the plea paperwork.

The next morning, Sean drove Carla over to the courthouse.
They met with the DA Samuels and went over the paperwork,
which mainly consisted of recognition of waivers of constitutional rights such as right to a jury trial, not to testify, and con-
frontation of witnesses. These protections would not be
necessary when you have an agreed plea and sentence.

When Sean, Samuels and Carla approached the bench,
Judge Treadway was not scowling and that was good thing. She
turned to Samuels first.

"Has the State offered a plea? What is it?"

"Three years of probation, a $5,000 fine, 50 hours of com-
munity service, and random urinalysis."

Judge Treadway looked at Sean who agreed to the terms.
Treadway leaned back. "It seems light for the amount of pot involved, but I accept it."

The judge read the various constitutional waivers and asked
Carla if she signed them, to which she assented. The judge finally asked for her plea of guilty, then sentenced her in accor-
dance with the agreement.

Sean then brought up the fact that the probation needed to be transferred to Kansas City. He knew that judges don't usually like to let people on probation out of their court leave the jurisdiction.

Judge Treadway was reasonable. "Due to her age and the short term of the probation, I will allow it."

After the plea, Carla went to meet with the court's probation personnel. Sean was killing time in the courtroom when the DA Samuels came over with two men in dark suits who had the obvious look of federal agents. Sean could usually pick them out by their cheap suits and haircuts. They both had the same sour demeanor.

The taller one said, "Agent Harris" and flashed his DEA credentials. Sean didn't even hear the other one when he flashed his badge. Harris said, "We would like to talk with your client Carla Miller."

Sean looked at the DA Samuels, who said "Don't know anything about this." With that he backed away.

Carla was approaching after completing her meeting with probation. Sean turned her around and went to talk with her in a corner.

"These guys are federal DEA agents. They want to talk with you. You can refuse to talk with them, but why don't we find out what they want?" Carla nodded.

Sean approached the agents and said, "Let's take this outside. There are some benches outside the courthouse doors." Moreover, it was a beautiful fall day in the Valley.

Carla and Sean immediately sat down on the bench outside. One agent joined them and the other remained standing.

Agent Harris started speaking. "We know that this case was not your only trip picking up marijuana and cocaine. There have been numerous other trips where you have delivered vehicles and then picked up a loaded car." He stopped and looked at Carla. Sean believed it was to see her reaction, which was impassive.

Harris continued. "The government is preparing to present an indictment for conspiracy to distribute marijuana and cocaine. You are one of the members of this conspiracy. The amounts we are alleging will make any punishment severe. This is why we are here to talk with you. If you agree to cooperate, then we can lessen any possible exposure."

Sean thought, if the agent had anticipated that this nice older lady would break down, he was sorely mistaken. Carla bowed up like a snake getting ready to strike.

"Fuck you. Fuck the government and fuck any deal." Carla's eyes were blazing with hatred.

Agent Harris did not seem prepared for this reaction. He stood and said to Sean, "You need to explain things to your client. Call me and we can talk." He handed Sean his embossed DEA business card. Harris and his shadow agent then left.

Carla turned to Sean. "What the hell was that? I thought this plea took care of my problems."

Sean looked at Carla. "It took care of the State of Texas case. The feds can always make a case as well. It sounds like they are framing a case to put together large quantities of coke and pot. They can make you responsible for drugs that you had no actual hand in delivering. If they prove you were part of a group delivering drugs, and you agreed to do it, then they have their case. The problem in federal drug cases is that the punishment goes up as the amount goes up.

"Now what is this about you delivering one car and picking up another? Is that true?"

Carla looked at her shoes and seemed to be deciding what to say. "Many times, the Valentis would bring me a vehicle, often a Lexus or Mercedes, and tell me to leave it at the hotel I would stay at in McAllen or Laredo. I would get keys for the car I would drive back at my hotel room. Those cars were usually a Buick or a Ford. I did not question anything. Actually, it made it much easier and I never met anyone."

Sean sat back and started piecing some information together. It could not be coincidence that both the Miami gangsters and the Kansas City family were involved with cars and dope in South Texas. It would not really matter unless they all were indicted together. Then Sean would have some real conflict of interest problems.

He told Carla that there was nothing to be done about the federal investigation and to return to Kansas City. Sean needed to get some more information from the Valentis, and maybe take a trip to Miami as well.

Chapter Six
Funeral II

The following day, Sean was in his office, catching up. Whenever he went out of town on a case, or fun, it seemed like there were always matters to address that were not around when he left. Of course, e-mails comprised the bulk of the work. This electronic messaging was both a boon and a bane to Sean's existence. One e-mail in particular caught his attention from the day before from a non-descript sender, but the subject line read simply: "Gus Valenti death."

Sean immediately switched to Google and ran "Gus Valenti." A stream of articles followed. Sean picked the *Kansas City Star* and read that the reputed boss of the Kansas City mafia died of an apparent heart attack.

Sean retrieved John Valenti's cell phone number from his case file and called him.

"John, I just heard about your father. My condolences. Is there anything I can do?"

"No, thanks anyway. I will text you information on the funeral. I would like it if you would attend."

"Of course. I will be there." Sean did not want to make a

habit of appearing at mafia funerals, but there was no way around this one.

Later that day Sean received an e-mail from a Mr. Orange. It said simply: "Our friend will see you in Kansas City." Sean was not surprised that Cicero would be going to the Valenti funeral, but how did he know Sean was going? There appeared to be more communication between Kansas City and Miami then he anticipated. It might make matters complicated for him.

When Sean arrived in Kansas City, and was walking toward the baggage claim area, he saw his name on a sign. He approached the man holding the sign, who was dressed in a black chauffeur outfit. Sean pointed at the sign and said, "That would be me."

The man smiled and told him, "I have been sent to be your ride for the Valenti funeral. Let's get your luggage and go to your hotel."

As they walked toward the luggage carousel, the driver told Sean that his name was Jordan. He regularly worked for the Valentis. He was a large man with a full head of black hair and looked the part of a driver/bodyguard.

After returning with the luggage, Jordan went to get the black Lincoln Town Car. Sean noted that he would fit right in with the other mob limos, Lincolns, and Cadillacs. As they traveled into downtown, Sean made small talk with Jordan, then realized he did not know where he was staying. John Valenti had insisted on lining up hotel accommodations. Jordan told Sean that he was staying at the Hyatt Regency downtown.

"There is a tragic tale of that hotel. In 1981, they were

sponsoring a party at the hotel and people were dancing on the suspended walkways. The walkways collapsed and more than one hundred people died." Jordan told this like a tourist guide.

Sean vaguely remembered reading about this tragedy and recalled his tort professor in law school using it as a case study of mass casualty damage claims. As the professor liked to say, bad luck for other people was good luck for lawyers. *Twisted, but true,* thought Sean.

When they arrived at the hotel, Jordan dropped Sean at the front door, and told him, "I will be here to pick you up tomorrow at ten." Sean thanked him and entered the hotel.

This Hyatt Regency was like most others with a huge open-air atrium. Sean eyed the walkaways crisscrossing the atrium at various levels and thought about the tragedy that occurred. *I am sure that these are now the best secured in the world. The positive to a large tort lawsuit is that it forces companies to foresee problems before they occur. Sometimes,* thought Sean, *but not always.*

Sean was placed on the concierge floor at the top of the hotel. The room was large and comfortable. He was hanging his clothes when there was a knock at the door. Sean opened the door to find Lou Cicero, who walked into the room and sat in one of the easy chairs in the room.

"Come join me." Sean took a seat in the adjacent chair.

Cicero started talking, something he rarely did when they met. "I have known the Valentis since I was a youngster. Gus Valenti, and his brother Augie, were like uncles to me. They would come to Jersey and always brought me something. A baseball glove signed by George Brett, a football signed by

Hank Stram, and almost always some Kansas City memorabilia. I appreciated the attention."

This was more than Cicero had ever talked about himself or his past. Sean was a little taken aback, but anxious to hear more.

Cicero continued. "As I started making my bones, I started doing things with the Kansas City family. In fact, the drug case you handled for me was related to them."

Sean had never had much background on the circumstances of the case since it was not relevant to his handling of the appeal, which dealt only with the sentence he received.

"The car deals you represented my guys on in Dallas is tied to the Valentis. We all have business interests in Houston and South Texas."

Cicero at this point stood up and crossed over to the bar against the wall. There were mini bottles of liquor on a shelf. He asked, "Can I get you one?" He poured a Chivas Regal into a glass.

Sean offered some ice that had been left in a bucket. Cicero declined, and Sean decided to pour a Johnnie Walker Black, with ice.

Cicero took a large gulp and then sat back down.

"I don't know if you are aware, but Houston is an open city. No one can restrict any Family member from doing business there. It is the only major city in America that is not controlled by a Family."

Sean had heard this before. It was "urban legend," but hearing it from Cicero made it real. The 'street word' was that one guy tried to form a family, and he was left in the trunk of his Caddy with his balls stuffed in his mouth.

"This is why the Valentis and my group joined together to do business in Texas. No one restricts the other. It is joint business. Each family sends a member who is responsible for the interest in Texas. John Valenti represented his family and my interest. I provided assistance as necessary." Cicero smiled and said, "You met some of my assistants in Dallas."

"Anyway, it is my hope that I will continue business with the Valentis, but I am not as familiar with Augie as I was with Gus. Augie will be the new boss."

Sean had not thought about the hierarchy of the Kansas City mafia, but it seemed logical that it would stay in the family.

Cicero took another gulp and finished his glass of scotch. "I felt you should know the dynamics of what you are representing and be prepared for possible conflicts."

Cicero stood and started toward the door. "I will see you at the funeral tomorrow. I have business tonight."

He exited the room and left Sean pondering what he had told him. It was not what he anticipated. The ties between Miami, Kansas City, and Houston were tightening.

The next morning, Sean put on his best dark gray suit, white shirt, and dark tie. He went to the lobby to meet Jordan and brought his suitcase to leave after the funeral and the obligatory meal.

Jordan drove Sean to a funeral home not far from downtown. When Sean entered the home, he saw the Valenti brothers greeting people. Standing with them was a tall, balding man who bore a strong resemblance to the brothers. *That must be Uncle Augie, the new capo,* thought Sean. He was introduced to Augie, provided his condolences, and then he walked up to David and John. He provided condolences, and as he was walking away, John grabbed his arm.

"We need to talk after the burial. There will be a gathering at a nearby Italian restaurant. Jordan will know the place."

Sean was going to tell him that his return flight was at five that afternoon, but then he realized John bought the tickets.

The funeral itself was fairly mundane. There were platitudes about what a great guy Gus Valenti was, and his community activities. Sean thought it was all probably bullshit, but you couldn't very well state that Gus was a sociopathic criminal boss. The better part of the ceremony highlighted Gus and his family ties. Both David and John gave heartfelt eulogies.

While this was transpiring, Sean looked around the crowded theater and tried to discern who comprised the assembled group. There were obvious mobsters, some capos from other families (like Cicero), and even some politicians. A contingent of Teamster officials were present with their Teamsters Union symbol on their sportscoats. The crowd was older and not many young faces were present.

The burial was in the adjoining cemetery. The group gathered by the enormous marble sculpture that was a cheap imitation of Michelangelo's "David." This was in lieu of a tombstone. The assembled group praised the grandiose sculpture, then splintered off to their respective vehicles. Sean walked back to Jordan's Continental, which was hidden in the midst of similar vehicles. It was a short drive to the Italian restaurant "Da Vinci."

As the name implied, the walks were adorned with frescoes

and paintings of Leonardo da Vinci's famous pieces: *The Last Supper,* his self-portrait, and of course, the *Mona Lisa.* The building itself was similar to a Roman villa. Although pretentious, it had the feel of an Italian restaurant.

Sean entered the restaurant and immediately headed for the bar. He did not know many of the assembled guests and figured his best place was on the sidelines to gauge the group. As frequently happens after a funeral, the group became loud and gregarious. Sean even saw Cicero drinking and being convivial. It helped that no one had their cell phones as well.

John and David Valenti were doing their duty visiting with one group after another. Soon the staff set up the buffet with pastas, meats, cheeses, and sauces. *No one will go hungry,* thought Sean.

Eventually, John Valenti made his way to Sean. Sean complimented him on the statue, and the Italian spread for the guests. John didn't seem to hear and ordered a shot of bourbon. He downed it and then asked Sean to accompany him outside for a cigarette.

After they were outside, Sean accepted one of the Marlboro Lights and joined John for a smoke.

"Tell me about the feds and Carla." John started this more as an instruction than a question.

Sean had anticipated that Carla would tell the Valentis what transpired, which made it easier for him to talk.

"Two federal agents from the DEA confronted us outside the state courthouse. They explained that there was a federal investigation ongoing regarding the transporting of marijuana and cocaine by a group that Carla was involved with. This is a conspiracy case and they are alleging Carla is a member of the conspiracy. She will be facing stiff penalties if they tie her to substantial quantities of coke or marijuana, even if she did not actually transport that much."

John looked concerned and took a drag on the cigarette. "Did they identify anyone else?"

Sean said, "No. They are not going to provide information now. They are seeking information. It doesn't take much imagination to discern who else might be involved."

Sean pointed at John with his cigarette and then put it out on the ground.

John was quiet then stated, "They knew about the cars we have been bringing as well, according to Carla."

Sean nodded. "I also know that Miami is involved as well."

John sighed. "Cicero told me a couple of his drivers went to the grand jury. So what is our exposure with Carla?'

"At this point, we wait on an indictment because I do not believe she will help the government."

John looked at the ground and dropped his cigarette. "It would not go well for me or my partners if she did."

John looked up and took Sean by the arm. "Let's go get some good food, then you can catch your flight. I will be back to Houston soon. I am looking for a high-rise condominium. Maybe you can suggest a realtor."

This caught Sean by surprise. He did not figure on John Valenti leaving Kansas City. Could there be other issues? Before Sean could question him further, they were in the restaurant and John was involved with family duties.

Sean ate some pasta, said his goodbyes to Cicero and the

brothers, and then left for the airport. As he watched the highway scenery roll by, he realized that he had not seen Carla at the funeral. That seemed odd, but she could have been lost in the crowd. He would follow up when he returned to the office.

Chapter Seven
Risky Business

Houston is a massive city with a very diverse population. It is reported to be the most diverse city in the United States. There are Vietnamese, Cambodians, South Asians (Pakistanis and Indians), Iranians, Africans, Russians, South and Central Americans, and, of course, Mexicans. There is one thing that all of these groups, as well as the black and white Americans, have in common—they all have organized crime groups that prey and protect their own ethnic groups. Of course, there is considerable economics interplay between the various groups.

Sean was fortunate to be the "go-to" lawyer for the Pakistani organized crime group, the Russian mafia, and some of the true American Italian Mafia families.

Along with the usual ruffians and drug dealers, Sean kept a busy practice. Although advertising was becoming the link for many lawyers, Sean found that personal referrals were the only way to develop a lucrative criminal practice. When the criminal honchos gave him a referral, it usually paid well, often by the referring group or individual.

Sean's main source of business was drug distribution

groups, primarily marijuana. There were many such groups in the nation and connected through Houston. It was with these groups and their tendrils throughout America that Sean had developed a nationwide practice. Most of these cases were in federal court and Sean could request "pro hac vice" status (to appear on just the one case) or pay a fee to join the local district. He had been admitted to the United States Supreme Court bar years before and this opened doors at all the federal districts from New York to Los Angeles. Sean enjoyed being the Texas lawyer in the various locales around the country and was usually afforded respect. Many court personnel were disappointed that Sean did not appear in cowboy boots and a bolo tie, although he did wear exotic boots on occasion (water buffalo, eel, or ostrich) to make a statement.

Since the Valenti funeral, Sean had been busy tending to his state criminal docket. Other than appearing in court, this entailed discovery of information from the State, investigating, drafting motions, and meeting with the clients and assistant district attorneys.

Sean's days were busy and his nights were becoming more sedate. He was seeing Janey on a fairly regular basis and tried to have dinner with her at least twice a week outside of the club. He wished that she would do something other than work at Foxies, but it was hard to argue with the money she made. She was investing, so she had a stable base for the next phase of her life. She could also pick up and leave with him for extended travels. Just prior to Abe's funeral, they had gone to France-Paris, the Loire Valley, Bordeaux, and the Riviera. Along with her other attributes, Janey was a good traveling companion.

Sean had just returned to the office from a particularly difficult day in court when he was flagged down by Maria.

"You have a potential client. He was picked up by the federal marshal's office on an indictment out of San Diego. You are to contact a Mr. Clement, who will fill you in."

Sean took the call slip and went into his office. When Sean returned the call, he was told that Peter Suh was being held by the United States Marshals in Houston on a federal drug conspiracy case out of San Diego. Sean knew that Mr. Suh would have an appearance in Houston federal court in the next day for identity purposes and to arrange transfer to San Diego. This would also be the time to get a bond, if possible. Mr. Clement (Sean figured not his real name) seemed aware of the pending deadlines. He said that an envelope would be delivered with a sufficient fee to handle matters in Houston federal court. Sean had not yet set a fee and did not like discussing fees on the phone. He told Mr. Clement that he would go to the federal detention center and see Mr. Suh. Sean also figured that if the fee was light, he could take it up later.

On the way out of the office, Sean told Maria to expect an envelope, and he picked up the information she had requested on Peter Suh from the federal clerk's office. The indictment was typical federal overkill, charging Peter Suh, along with others whose names were blackened out, with a conspiracy to distribute heroin between Houston, Texas and San Diego, California. Moreover, the amounts were significant—in the hundreds of kilos.

Sean disliked the federal detention centers in Houston. One was about thirty miles from downtown and the other in the middle of downtown. They both had a cold, sterilized feel, almost like a hospital. The procedure to get in was rigorous. Your identity as an attorney licensed in the federal court was checked. No cell phones allowed. Any briefcases are x-rayed and the lawyers had to pass through a scanner as well.

Once inside, the lawyer would be assigned a cubicle to talk with the client. This was a small cubicle with a metal chair on either side of a plexiglass partition. This is where Sean waited for Mr. Suh to appear. About fifteen minutes later, the door to the other side of the partition opened and a tall, nice-looking man entered. He looked Eurasian, a mix of Asian features with an American body type.

"My name is Sean Braxton. I am a criminal defense attorney in Houston. I was contacted to try and assist you in the detention matter here on an indictment out of San Diego." Peter Suh nodded his assent.

"I would prefer we keep matters general in here because there may be government ears in this room. Despite the assurances that these rooms are sacrosanct for attorney-client discussions, I don't trust the government." Peter Suh smiled.

"I am not seeking any explanation from you. Have you been shown the indictment? Good. My immediate concern is demonstrating that you are not a threat to public safety or a flight risk. Tell me about yourself and your family, business, and so on."

Peter Suh explained that he owned an export-import business which worked out of the Houston Ship Channel, the largest port by tonnage in America. He was forty-five years old, with two kids in high school, and living in a nice residential area called Bellaire. He noted that he had numerous business contracts in California but was at a loss to explain the drug conspiracy charge. Peter Suh provided contact information for his wife and business partner.

Sean explained that he would charge $10,000 for the detention proceedings in Houston, but considerably more for the actual case in California. Sean explained that he had been contacted by Mr. Clement. Peter seemed to be aware of this and stated that the envelope being delivered should be sufficient.

Sean took his leave of Peter Suh, telling him that he would see him in court, and returned to his office. The envelope had been delivered with exactly $10,000. Sean had a feeling that Mr. Suh and his partners were versed in dealing with lawyers on similar matters. Sean got busy immediately, contacting character witnesses, and having Maria find out all she could about Mr. Suh's business, Dragon Imports.

The next morning, Sean was in the Federal Building in downtown Houston for the bond hearing on Mr. Suh. The Federal Building was generally recognized as the ugliest building in the downtown area. It was a cube of white stone material with small square windows. However, the layout inside was a sharp contrast to the architectural vulgarity of the outside. The district courthouses were large, wood encased shrines to justice. There were immense columns on either side of the judge's bench perched high above the rest of the courtroom. This design only reinforced the old idiom that the only power greater than a federal district judge was God, and even that might be questioned by members of the bar.

Bond hearings were traditionally heard by magistrates, who

were assigned by the federal judges to handle detention matters. The magistrate on Suh's case was Tracy Gillums. She was known as a compassionate and knowledgeable judge, which Sean believed could work in their favor.

Sean met with Vivian Suh, the attractive and articulate wife. She was from Singapore, and had that thin, graceful look of a model. It was her role to present the stable family portrait for the judge.

Frank Stamos was Suh's business partner. He was dressed in an expensive suit and looked the part of the business executive. As it turned out, Stamos was a financial partner in the business, but was not involved in the day to day running of the business. Mr. Stamos portrayed himself as an investor involved in an assortment of businesses.

Just before the judge took the bench at 10 A.M., the three of them made it to the magistrate's courtroom, which was not as grand as the district court. Representing the government was Joe Paggione, as assistant United States attorney, with whom Sean was quite familiar and friendly. Joe walked over to Sean and handed him a copy of the indictment, which Sean had been unable to access because it had been sealed.

Federal conspiracy indictments frequently cite to other co-conspirators, who are blacked out if not arrested. This was the case in Peter Suh's indictment. The government was alleging that Peter Suh, through Dragon Imports, was importing the narcotic drug fentanyl. Although used medically, it was known to be added as an ingredient to low concentration heroin to make it stronger. Peter Suh was alleged to have shipped the drug to San Diego, where it had been incorporated into heroin being sold by a known Vietnamese drug gang. The indictment also alleged a few deaths related to the heroin. (Fentanyl could kill with only a few grains, which made it inherently dangerous.)

Sean knew that this was a hot issue with the government and the public because of the opioid "epidemic" in America. When Peter Suh was led into the courtroom prior to the judge taking the bench, Sean went over to the marshals to have him segregated from the other prisoners so they could talk. When they were off to the side, Sean showed that indictment to Peter.

"Do you import fentanyl?"

Peter looked up from the indictment. "Yes. We have licenses from the FDA and the DEA."

"Who are your customers?"

"Drugstores and hospitals, predominately. If they present the paperwork, then we are authorized to sell. It does not say who I sent it to."

Sean noted, "I saw that immediately. The government blacked out the names and they may claim they have the right until all parties are arrested. The government will have to produce some testimony on the subject today and I will try to get some more information. By the way, can your partner, Frank Stamos, testify about importing fentanyl?"

Peter shook his head in assent. "It has been a lucrative part of the business."

Just as they concluded their conversation, Judge Gillums took the bench and Sean went back to the counsel table.

After the usual decorum of a federal judge taking the bench, (concluding with "God save this Court and United States"), Judge Gillums stated: "We have some preliminary matters and then we will get to the detention hearing on Peter Suh."

This allowed Sean some time to go talk with Frank Stamos, who stated that he knew that Dragon Imports brought fentanyl from China and distributed it nationwide. Since the company had all the correct government approval, what was the problem? Sean had to point out that he was still not clear on the government's angle but planned to find out.

After Sean and Frank re-entered the courtroom, the judge was handling other matters related to other prisoners. About a half-hour later, Judge Gillums called the Peter Suh case.

Just prior to starting the hearing, Joe Paggione asked permission of the court to talk briefly with Sean.

Judge Gillums said, "Make it real brief."

Joe pulled Sean to the side and said he would agree to a $20,000 bond. This was unusual in a drug case.

Sean said, "I appreciate your offer, but I think we need to see what the point of this indictment is. I am hoping your agent can shed some light on things."

Joe nodded and said, "With the possibility of detention without bond, you might want to reconsider."

"Let me ask my client."

Sean went back to the counsel table where Peter Suh was now sitting. He explained the offer and said that there was a risk the judge could hold him, but this would be the chance to find out what is going on. Sean also felt the judge would give them a bond anyway, but it was a risk. Peter agreed and Sean shook his head no to Joe.

Judge Gillums recognized Sean's negative head shake and

said, "Is the government ready to proceed?"

Joe stated, "Yes, your honor. The government calls FBI agent Mark McMullen."

As the agent went to the stand, Sean had to curtail his surprise. It was not usual in a drug case that the agent would be FBI and not DEA.

After the usual introductory questions on Agent McMullen's position, years with the government, and current station, Joe got to the point.

"Are you familiar with the defendant Peter Suh?"

"Yes, I am. He is the owner and operator of Dragon Imports."

"Why is that significant?"

Agent McMullen shifted in his seat to talk to the judge. "Dragon Imports brings fentanyl to the United States from China."

Joe asked the agent, "How is that relevant in this indictment?"

Agent McMullen became very serious. "There is a DEA informant in San Diego who provided information that Dragon Imports sent fentanyl to a member of the Emperor Kings drug group. They are a Vietnamese gang, your Honor."

Sean interrupted, "Objection. Speculation and hearsay."

Judge Gillums said, "I will allow it for this Hearing."

Joe now asked, "Is there any information that corroborates this informant's statements?"

Agent McMullen looked down at a file he had carried to the witness stand.

"Yes. First, we found records that Dragon Imports sent one

kilogram of fentanyl to an EK Medical Supply in San Diego. The San Diego drug enforcement officer stated that this medical supply is a known front for the Emperor King's organization.

"Second, there was some fentanyl recovered in a heroin bust with known Emperor King members. The fentanyl was still in packaging indicating it was the same fentanyl shipped to EK Medical Supply."

Joe asked, "How does this involve Peter Suh?"

The agent turned to the judge. "He is one of the owners of Dragon Imports and is the manager of operations. Oh, and it was his signature on bill of lading on the fentanyl shipped to San Diego." He said this last sentence with a measure of arrogance.

Joe now asked the agent, "Is there any other information that raised any suspicion on Dragon Imports?"

Agent McMullen puffed up in his seat. "The other owner of Dragon Imports is Frank Stamos and he is a known affiliate of the Valenti crime family in Kansas City."

Sean had to control his emotions to not register surprise. Time to keep composure.

"The government passes the witness." Joe smiled at Sean, knowing that he had caught him off-guard.

Sean took a minute to look at his notes, but basically to get his head around these events. He began the cross-examination of the FBI agent.

"Agent McMullen, Dragon Imports has both FDA and DEA licenses to import fentanyl, isn't that right?"

"Yes, that is true."

"And it is their business to distribute what they import?"

"Of course."

"Did EK Medical Supply have a DEA license to receive and distribute fentanyl?

"As far as I can tell, yes."

"Is there any information that would be available to the public that EK Medical Supply was anything other than what its name implies?"

Agent McMullen shifted in his chair. "Other than some of the individuals working at EK Medical Supplies had prior drug convictions, probably not."

Sean said, "If there were unauthorized persons, that is something the licensed authorities need to address, right?"

"I suppose."

"Any information that Mr. Suh knew anything about the criminal backgrounds of the employees?"

"No."

Sean started feeling confident. "So, this case is built on an informant's statement that relies on speculation for any verification."

"I don't believe so."

Sean changed course. "Because you contend that an investor in Dragon Imports is associated with another alleged criminal organization?"

"Yes, in part."

"And any alleged connections to the Valenti crime gang is based on other agent's reports or observations?"

Agent McMullen looked confused. "So, that is usual."

Sean took a chance to go fishing here. "However, it is based on hearsay that you cannot corroborate, correct?"

Agent McMullen did not answer, and the judge leaned towards him and said, "We need an answer."

McMullen finally said, "I cannot corroborate the reports."

"Thank you, officer. Defense passes the witness." .

At this stage, Sean knew he could not put Frank Stamos on for any reason. He called the wife and established that Peter Suh was a father with strong attachments to Houston.

The government argued that there was a presumption of detention in a large drug case and bond should be denied.

As Sean got up to argue, the judge said, "Save your breath, counselor. The government has barely made a prima facie showing of cause. I am going to authorize a personal recognizance bond. Mr. Suh, get with the pretrial people in the court."

With a sideways look at the Assistant United States attorney, Joe Paggione, the judge left the bench.

Sean explained to Mr. Suh and his wife that he was free on bond for no money, until an appearance was required in San Diego. As Sean was getting ready to leave the courtroom, Joe Paggione came over.

"Do you have a minute to talk Sean?"

Sean agreed and they went out in the corridor.

Joe turned to Sean and said, "I am going to handle the case with your client Carla Miller. I expect an indictment within the next month. I again want to offer her a get out of jail free card with her testimony."

Sean replied, "I do not think she is inclined to go there."

Joe got serious. "That is too bad. I think that we will get an indictment on John Valenti as well. You know it's funny how you seem to be around whenever Valenti people are the accused."

Sean shrugged and said, "Just lucky I guess."

As Joe walked away, he said, "Better try to steer clear of conflicts."

Sean knew that this was his next problem.

Chapter Eight
Conflict Resolution

As Sean drove back to the office, he reflected on how all these recent cases have one common denominator: John Valenti. He was involved in many different illegal activities, but they all seemed to be linked to Houston and South Texas. Sean also realized that, as the federal prosecutor observed, he was heading for obvious conflicts of interest that could prevent him from representing Valenti. Sean called John Valenti from his car phone. As it turned out, Valenti was in Houston, so they set a meeting for later that day.

At three that afternoon, Valenti was in Sean's office. Sean had him sit in the traditional client chairs across from his desk. This needed to be as formal as possible.

"John, I asked you here to talk about your role in the cases I am handling in South Texas, you are obviously intertwined with Carla's federal case, which will soon have indictments. I expect you to be included. Needless to say, I cannot represent you and her."

John started to break in, but Sean held up his hand. "Let me go into the other issues that I see you being involved in. First, there is your role with the state's case that was presented to a grand jury in Dallas. Second, I found out after the hearing today that you are involved with the importation and distribution of fentanyl. If you are charged in any of the cases, I may be prevented from representing you."

John nervously said, "Why is that?"

Sean realized he was at the edge of his seat, so he slid back and took a deep breath. "A lawyer cannot represent two people who are charged in the same criminal episode. The problem is that what might be advantageous for one party could be harmful to the other party. Furthermore, there is a real problem if one party decides to cooperate with the government to help their case and would necessarily hurt the other party."

John loudly said, "That ain't gonna happen with Carla. Those guys with the cars in Dallas don't know nothing about my role. Finally, I am a back seat player on the fentanyl. That is Frank Stamos."

"Yes, but you are high profile. From the government lawyer's viewpoint, any role you have makes the case sexier."

John smiled, "Nice to know I have some sex appeal. I am glad you called me today because I was going to see you anyway." John stopped and lowered his voice to a whisper. "I am moving my center of operations to Houston. My uncle wants to take the family in one direction, and I want to go in another. My brother will deal with my uncle.

"Anyway, I have purchased a high-rise condominium in the Galleria area to live in and I bought a small office park to center my business. That is why I want to talk to you." John hesitated then said, "I want you to be my Counsel to advise me as I go forward. It will pay much more than a law practice."

Sean was taken aback by this request. He did not want to get in bed with a gangster at this stage of his career, even for untold wealth. It was Sean's goal to be a defense lawyer and try to ethically represent those persons charged with crimes, not be part of the criminal world. However, it would not look good for him to decline right away. Better to buy time.

"I need to think about this John. But I do have one question, are you starting a new family in Houston? Isn't there an unwritten rule that Houston remains an open city?'

John shifted in his chair. "I am not declaring a separate family here. I am just centering my enterprise out of here."

"Are you sharing with Kansas City?"

John replied immediately, "But of course. For now."

Sean decided to let that issue stay. "The immediate concern is my representation of Carla and your possible prosecution in South Texas."

John looked sullen. "That is concerning. Well, let me know what you think about my offer." He rose and extended his hand to Sean, who shook it.

John added as he walked out the door. "It will work out."

That night, Sean had a date with Janey. He drove to her bungalow in one of the bohemian areas of Houston called Montrose. It was a picturesque little house with verdant gardens around it. The giant elephant ears, ginger, and the fragrant angel trumpets gave the place a very tropical feel. Sean's only hesitancy was parking his Corvette on the street all night, fearing he would find it gone or on blocks.

Janey was dressed in a form fitting red dress that accented her figure and complemented her strawberry blonde hair. Sean drove them to one of his favorite bistro restaurants in an old house in Montrose. The food was usually superb, there was a good wine list, and you could usually get a private table away from curious listeners.

After they seated at a table and selected a bottle of Pinot Noir, Sean opened the conversation with Janey regarding his offer from John Valenti. She was aware of who Valenti was but not any particulars. Sean began, "I was approached about being an adviser to John Valenti. It would be a lot of money, but I don't want to be in bed with a mobster. The problem is that turning down the offer could be seen as an offense to Valenti."

The waiter appeared at this point and brought the bottle of Pinot Noir. After acknowledging Sean's approval, the waiter poured two glasses. As soon as the waiter left, Janey said, "Why do you even need to consider this? You already have a ticket to make a good living. Why risk it?"

Sean smiled at her. "It is not that I am without a criminal past. There was a time period where I was actively involved with distributing marijuana. I don't mean selling ounces, but arranging to ship hundreds of pounds to ports in the U.S.

"Remember when I told you about my house in Jamaica. Well, this house was situated on the western end of Jamaica in a place called Negril. There were sea caves that could be used to store marijuana from Colombia and even the mountains of Jamaica.

"Everything was packaged in watertight plastic wraps. Speedboats came from big ships going to Florida, New Orleans, and Houston. They picked up the pot and delivered it to the ships. It was easy and relatively safe. The problem was the Jamaican authorities found out and I just avoided being prosecuted or executed. After I got out, I swore that was not the life for me."

Janey looked shocked. "I never figured you for a drug trafficker. Did you at least make some money?"

"Well, it did pay for most of my college and law school. The other added benefit was opening me up to many of the people in the marijuana trade, so that I had a roster of clients when I hung out my shingle." Sean smiled and took a large swig of his wine.

"Anyway, that is why I am not interested in going back to the dark side."

Janey looked at Sean. "You need to phrase any rejection of this offer so that your client sees it as an affirmation of your looking out for his interest. He can hardly be upset if you are looking out for him."

Sean realized that she had hit on an angle that would provide a simple solution. "You are right. Valenti wants me close so that I have to represent him. So long as I can play that hand, it should work." Sean leaned over and kissed Janey on the lips. "I knew that talking with you would help me. Let's order some food."

The next day, Sean reached out to John Valenti, who was traveling but said he would be back in a couple of days.

This was good because Sean needed some time to get more of his docket straightened out. There were police reports to review, videos of traffic stops, and being a steady voice for the clients uneasy in the role as a defendant. Sean liked to describe his job as part sleuth (like Sherlock Holmes); part academic (sifting through the law books); part therapist (dealing with the many mental issues prevalent with criminals); and finally, part actor when the case goes to trial. Balancing all these roles could be time consuming and tiring. In fact, Sean felt more tired after a full day with clients than he used to feel after ten hours of heavy labor as a Teamster. It is just part of the game, he told himself.

It was while he was working at the office sorting through his files that he received a call from Joe Paggione, the federal prosecutor.

"Hi Sean. I am giving you a heads-up that Carla was indicted by a Houston grand jury. The case is going to be in Houston because much of the activity on the conspiracy was centered from here. You can bring Carla in to the U.S. Marshals office and we can do the initial appearance. I will not oppose a bond for her."

Sean had been anticipating this.

"She poses no threat, so it's a no brainer. Did you indict John Valenti?"

"Yes, but I oppose a bond on him. You are also going to have tough time representing both Carla and Valenti."

Sean said, "Don't worry. He will get someone to represent him."

"Let me know when you can bring Carla into the marshals. And Valenti too."

"Thanks, Joe. I will get back to you."

Shortly after this phone call, Sean reached out to both Carla and Valenti. Carla said that she had to get some affairs in order before she came down to Houston to surrender. Valenti said that he would come by Sean's office in the next couple of days to discuss strategy on the surrender. Sean reminded Valenti that he could get arrested at any time with a federal warrant outstanding.

Two days later, John Valenti showed up at Sean's office. When Sean saw him, he knew something was up.

Valenti sat heavily into the client chair across Sean's desk. "I have some bad news. Carla was killed by a hit and run driver in Kansas City."

Sean sat back in his chair, shocked at news. "When did this happen?"

"Yesterday afternoon. Carla was walking in her neighborhood, and she was hit by a car. One of the neighbors found her in a ditch."

Sean had been preparing the speech he planned to give Valenti regarding his conflict with representing Carla and him. He further planned on rejecting the offer to be his counsel.

Valenti added, almost as if he read Sean's mind. "I don't want to be morbid, but Carla's death removes any impediment to your representation of me in this case. Further, that other deal we talked about needs to be put off for now."

Sean was shocked both at John Valenti's callous demeanor and his conniving intent. Then again, Sean could not be that shocked at such reactions from an underworld capo. This also reinforced Sean's feeling that the Valentis were involved with

Carla's death, even though she was a long-time loyal employee.

Sean asked, "Is there a service planned yet?"

Valenti responded immediately. "The Teamsters local will pay for the funeral and give some pension funds to the family that Carla had coming. I will provide all the details when I know them."

Just then, Sean's receptionist buzzed into his phone. "Joe Paggione from the United States Attorney's Office is calling you on line two."

Sean looked at Valenti and held his finger up to his lips, so he would keep quiet. Sean punched the line two button.

"Sean, this is Joe Paggione. Are you aware that Carla Miller was killed yesterday?"

Sean replied, "I was just informed."

"How did you get the information?"

"Contacts from Kansas City let me know."

"This certainly makes it easier for you to represent John Valenti."

"That is cold, even from an old government lawyer. Let's show some respect for the dead."

"Do you think John Valenti will show respect? In fact, I have asked the Kansas City FBI to assist the local cops in their investigation. Her death seems too coincidental." Joe hesitated then said, "We still need to get John Valenti surrendered. When were you planning on doing that?"

Sean sensed a trap in where this conversation was going." I was in the process of working with Mr. Valenti to get other representation. At this stage, that seems to be unnecessary. I will contact Valenti and see if we can surrender tomorrow morning for an afternoon appearance docket."

Joe said, "You need to know I will ask for detention with no bond." With that, the line went dead.

Sean looked over at Valenti and summarized his discussion." We are going to need information on your employment and ties to the Kansas City community. I think we will avoid bringing up your planned relocation to Houston at this time."

Sean continued, "Just beware that you will probably be held in federal detention until we can have a hearing in a couple days."

Valenti stood up. "I guess I need to take care of a few things before I surrender tomorrow. Just make sure this detention is not for long." Valenti said this almost like an order, not a request. He left the office and picked up his phone from Maria. Sean could sense that the representation of John Valenti would be very difficult.

The next morning, Sean met John Valenti at the United States Courthouse in downtown Houston. Sean went with Valenti to the United States Marshal's office. One of the marshals came out to the lobby and escorted Valenti back to do the identification procedures. Sean told him as he headed back that he would see him at two in the magistrate courtroom.

Now that Sean was going to be representing John Valenti, he needed to resolve the conflict with Peter Suh and Dragon Imports. Sean met with Mr. Suh at his office and explained that there was going to be a conflict in his further representation. Sean knew an excellent criminal defense lawyer in San Diego named Paul Grant and he was referring Peter Suh to him. To give Peter confidence, Sean arranged a conference phone call with Grant. Sean could see that Peter Suh developed a rapport with Paul and they scheduled a meeting for next week. Sean explained to Peter that he had to be out of the loop, until they knew whether Valenti would become a defendant.

After the meeting with Suh, Sean ate a sandwich picked up by Maria, and then drove back to the federal courthouse.

The initial appearance was basically to ensure that the government had the right person in custody who was indicted by the grand jury, and to determine bond status. In John Valenti's case, the government, through Assistant United States Attorney Joe Paggione objected to a bond and moved for detention. The magistrate, John Brown, then set a detention hearing for two days later, on Friday at 10 A.M.

Over the next two days, Sean was busy putting together evidence to refute the government's presumption of danger to the community. This presumption was a vestige of the War on Drugs from President Reagan's time and basically equated large amounts of drugs with being a danger to the community. This meant that a federal judge or magistrate could then deny bond.

John Valenti's brother David came to Houston to assist on the case. Sean was presented documentation that the brothers had a lucrative trucking business hauling construction materials, oil and gas pipe, and even produce. Although the business was centered in Kansas City, Houston was also a hub. Of course, the close relationship with the Teamsters helped keep the labor issues to a minimum, and the profit margin healthy.

Sean intended to use David as a witness for John. David looked stable with a wife and kids. John had neither. Although

John had a prior cocaine case, David had no prior convictions.

At the hearing on Friday, the government attorney, Joe Paggione presented the indictment, which alleged the importation and distribution of hundreds of kilos of cocaine and marijuana.

The government used DEA agent Phil Harris to summarize the case. This was the same agent Sean met in South Texas, after Carla's hearing.

Agent Harris presented testimony that Carla had been arrested with 500 pounds of marijuana, that she worked with the Valenti's at the Teamsters office in Kansas City, and that she had been making frequent trips for marijuana and cocaine. Then Joe Paggione asked, "What happened with Carla Miller?"

Agent Harris said, "She was killed a few days ago in a hit and run in Kansas City."

Paggione asked, "Any information on what occurred?"

Harris replied, "Certainly convenient for John Valenti when we were going to offer immunity to testify against him."

Sean jumped to his feet, "Objection. Speculation."

Magistrate Brown agreed. "Unless there is something to tie John Valenti to her death, I will not consider it."

Paggione decided to change tactics. "Agent Harris what information do you have on John Valenti's role in the distribution of the marijuana?"

"There is an informant who provided testimony that John Valenti was in charge of receiving and ordering the distribution of both cocaine and marijuana from South Texas into Houston and Kansas City. He stated that hundreds of kilos were involved while he worked with the group."

"Specifically, what did the informant say the role of John

Valenti was in this conspiracy?"

Harris pulled out a notebook. "He stated that John Valenti put in the orders for the marijuana and cocaine with the San Miguel Cartel members in the Texas border towns of Brownsville, McAllen, and Laredo. He then sent people to pick up the drugs in previously loaded cars. He also had the drivers deliver top end cars to the Valley when they picked up the loaded vehicles."

Paggione asked, "What type of top end cars?"

"Mercedes, Lexus, and Cadillacs with altered titles. These cars were usually picked up in Houston or Dallas."

Paggione continued, "You mentioned the San Miguel Cartel. Are there any members you have identified as being involved in this endeavor?"

"Yes, sir. Saul Carrera and Pedro Soliz. They are both named in the indictment and are high ranking members of the group. Carrera is known as 'Snake Eyes' and is reputed to be the head of the cartel."

"Is there any other information that ties John Valenti to these people?"

Agent Harris again referred to his notebook. "Yes, a Texas DPS trooper seized a note from John Valenti's wallet when he stopped him in Laredo. The paper had the private cell number for Saul Carrera."

Paggione then asked, "Is the San Miguel Cartel known to the DEA?"

"Yes, sir. We have followed them for years and are familiar with their importation of marijuana, cocaine, and heroin through the Texas border. They have also been involved with putting fentanyl into the cocaine and heroin to make it stronger. This allows them to use diluted cocaine and heroin and increases profits. I would also add, it makes it deadlier as well."

Paggione took his seat and said, "Pass the witness."

Sean rose to cross examine the agent. "If I understood you, the only corroborating evidence for the informant's claims tying Mr. Valenti to the cartel members is a piece of paper with a phone number, is that right?"

"There is also the arrest of Valenti's former employee, Carla Miller, with five hundred pounds of marijuana."

"To be clear, Agent Harris, Carla Miller was a former employee of the Teamsters local in Kansas City, not to John Valenti. Yes or No?"

"Splitting hairs, counsel."

"Agent Harris, answer yes or no to the previous question."

"Yes, she worked for the Teamsters."

Sean realized that there was not much more he could do with this agent, except to ask the obvious questions. "No one from law enforcement ever seized any narcotics from the personal possession of John Valenti, did they?"

"No, sir."

"In fact, Agent Harris, despite your informant's claims, there are no actual seizures of marijuana or cocaine tied to this alleged conspiracy, other than five hundred pounds connected to Carla Miller?"

Agent Harris glared at Sean, and was hesitant to speak, until the magistrate said, "Agent Harris, please answer the question."

"There were no seizures, but surveillance confirmed much of what the informant stated."

Sean looked at John Valenti who nodded. "No further questions from defense, your Honor."

Paggione stood and informed the court that the government had met its burden for the statutory presentation of danger due to the amount of drugs involved, and also noted John Valenti's previous cocaine conviction.

Sean stated, "Your Honor, we would like to point out that this is a dry conspiracy, with no seized drugs other than the five hundred pounds of marijuana, which is not of sufficient quantity to instigate the statutory presumption.

"Further, we are prepared at this time to present evidence that Mr. Valenti is a businessman from Kansas City with strong community involvement."

Sean called David Valenti to the stand, and walked him through John's community involvement, his long-term Teamsters affiliation, and the trucking company that the two brothers owned. David made a good witness and looked more like a Little League coach than a fearsome member of the Mafia. Sean was surprised when Paggione scored almost no points on cross other than the family reputation.

John Valenti had provided information to Pre-Trial Services prior to the hearing so that they could verify Valenti's occupation with the trucking company and the Teamsters. Pre-Trial Services acted like the investigative arm of the Court and provided a report on the defendant. They also gave a recommendation on bond and suggested a $250,000 bond for Valenti with ten percent cash and a co-signer.

Sean and Paggione each made brief closing statements, but they knew the magistrate had made his mind up.

Magistrate Brown decided that a bond would be granted. He did state, "I believe that this case demonstrates criminal organizations at work, but the government's case needs more support. I will grant the $250,000 bond with ten percent deposit. I will also ask David Valenti to sign as a guarantor."

Of course, David agreed, and he arranged to pay the $25,000 that afternoon. John Valenti would walk out of the federal detention facility by the next morning.

Sean had told David to tell his brother when he picked him up that we needed to meet soon. Sean was going to secure the discovery evidence from the government to assess the case. Then he needed to meet with John Valenti and assess who the informant was, and how much he could provide to the government. Time for damage control, thought Sean. At least his conflicts appeared to have been settled.

There was a nagging feeling in his brain that John Valenti, and probably David Valenti, were more dangerous that Sean had figured. The ties to the fentanyl, which was killing thousands in America, was one problem. However, the killing of 75-year-old Carla Miller, by all accounts a close associate, seemed sociopathic and unnecessary.

Sean believed Carla would have gone to jail for the Valentis and would never have cooperated. It was evident to Sean that everyone around the Valentis was expendable, including him.

Chapter Nine
Disclosures

Over the next couple of days, Sean decided to investigate the factual scenarios intertwining with the prosecution of John Valenti.

First on the agenda, from a personal perspective, was ascertaining what happened with Carla Miller. Sean was able to talk with her daughter, who seemed to believe that her mother's death was not related to the Valentis. She noted that her mother took frequent walks in the neighborhood and there were no sidewalks in the semi-rural suburbs of Kansas City. Moreover, a description by a neighbor of the driver who hit her mother was one of a darker skinned man, not Black, but probably Hispanic, and driving a pickup truck.

Sean extended his condolences and apologized for not going to the funeral due to business concerns. He did send a large floral arrangement for the funeral.

The timing of the hit and run, and even the idea of a Hispanic driver, just seemed too coincidental. Sean knew that the cartel, and the Valentis, did not want a vulnerable asset like Carla that the government could use.

Sean also contacted Paul Grant, the San Diego criminal defense lawyer now representing Peter Suh. Although Grant had only done preliminary work investigating the government's case, he had discovered some interesting connections between the San Diego groups receiving the fentanyl and the San Miguel Cartel. This was set out in a couple of DEA reports he reviewed. Grant noted that there was not any hard evidence tying John Valenti to the transactions in San Diego. The problem was Frank Stamos' interest in Dragon Imports and his affiliation with John Valenti.

Sean had an uneasy feeling with the San Miguel Cartel being involved with Dragon Imports. It appeared to Sean that John Valenti, and probably David Valenti as well, were in bed with the San Miguel Cartel. He had to wonder how much the Kansas City Family knew about this alliance or was this a deal solely by the brothers. Sean also figured the government was trying to ascertain the same thing.

Two weeks after the bond hearing on John Valenti, Sean was granted access to the government's reports and evidence against Valenti. To accomplish this, Sean had to travel into downtown Houston to the offices of the United States Attorney for the Southern District of Texas. These offices were five floors in a high-rise skyscraper. After taking the elevator to the 24th floor, he was required to go through protective screening and pass through a metal detector. Then, he waited in a seating area and was escorted to a room with no windows where the files were arranged for him.

Sean settled into the stiff office chair provided. Although he could not prove it, Sean believed that the government produced its discovery in the most uncomfortable circumstances possible—stiff chair, no windows, and warm.

There were seven files on the table, each approximately three inches thick with reports. Sean perused each of the files before he started his in-depth review, and he noticed one salient factor, that there were reports from the FBI, DEA, and even the FDA. There were a lot of agencies in this fight, which was not usually the case.

The FBI reports dealt with John Valenti and his role in the Kansas City mafia family. There was his father's obituary and photos of the funeral with identifying tags for the other alleged mafia bosses. Front and center in one of the photos was Lou Cicero. There was even a photo of Sean, looking appropriately unhappy.

Much of the information included in the FBI file went to the business interests of the Valentis: unions, trucking, loan sharking, gambling, prostitution, and drugs. Many of the reports on the drugs noted John Valenti and his ties to Houston and South Texas, then referred to DEA reports.

As he expected, when Sean reviewed the FDA reports, the central object was Dragon Imports and the investor, Frank Stamos, with alleged ties to the Valentis. Nothing appeared in the reports about irregularities in the sale of the fentanyl. Sean needed to tell the San Diego attorney Grant about this record, because there were often gaps in what was provided by the government.

It was the DEA reports that had the motherlode of information. These reports (called a DEA-6) detailed the information provided by the informants, along with surveillance of various "persons of interest."

Sean was expecting the first report to detail the seizure of the five-hundred pounds of marijuana from Carla Miller, but there were numerous reports pre-dating her arrest.

The reports start in Laredo and detail how Valenti crime family members are regularly purchasing marijuana and cocaine from San Miguel Cartel figures. This informant was specific on meetings that John Valenti had with 'Snake Eyes,' the head of the cartel. More importantly, this informant seemed to know that Valenti brought $500,000 in cash to the cartel for cocaine that had been picked up.

This informant also detailed how the Valentis would deliver top-end cars, like Mercedes, Lexus, and Cadillacs, as payment on drug shipments. He also knew that the cartel would pre-package the marijuana or cocaine into older vehicles to be returned to Houston or Kansas City.

The reports also detailed how John Valenti would utilize Houston as a hub to distribute drugs. Many of the loaded vehicles went to the Valentis' trucking warehouse and then was transferred to trucks taking the drugs to various other cities. Sean realized this utilization of the Houston warehouse was how the government could bring its case in the Houston federal court rather than in the Laredo federal court.

As Sean reviewed the reports, it became obvious that no drugs had been seized other than the marijuana from Carla. This seemed to indicate that the informant was not privy to all the deliveries and pick-ups or there surely would have been more dope seized. Although there were details by the informant on kilo amounts on the cocaine and the marijuana, it could have been on the receiving end at the Houston or Kansas City warehouses.

There were also reports on the San Miguel Cartel, noting their involvement with marijuana, cocaine, and heroin distribution. Their point of sale was traditionally the border area of Texas. The cartel would bring it across and buyers would move it from there. There did not seem to be any information on heroin purchases by the Valentis. The use of fentanyl by the Cartel was mentioned, and then there was mention of Dragon Imports, but no direct connection. *This must be out of the informant's range of involvement,* thought Sean.

As he was finishing reading the last of the folders, the government lawyer Joe Paggione showed up. Sean had always liked Joe and believed he was an honest prosecutor, which was not always the case. Joe had a friendly face, balding with a quick smile, and Harry Potter round glasses. People instinctively liked him, which is why he was dangerous to the defense bar in front of juries.

Sean started the conversation, "There are only three defendants in this conspiracy case along with the 'unindicted co-conspirators.' Is that right?" The government frequently used unindicted co-conspirators to round out the conspiracy allegations, for example, people who loaded the drugs, moved the cars, and so on.

"That is all we need and it keeps the spotlight on your client." Joe smiled as he said this.

Sean continued, "The other two defendants are in the San Miguel Cartel and living in Mexico. They will never see the inside of a courtroom for this case. Besides, they have been indicted before and, from what I know, have never been arrested on the outstanding warrants. So your only other target was Carla

Miller, and your plan was to flip her against Valenti. With her untimely demise, your case is looking like an 'all for nothing' with your informant."

Joe shrugged his shoulders. "You play 'em as you get 'em. By the way, I heard from homicide in Kansas City. They found the vehicle believed to have run down Carla. It was a late model Chevy truck and had been torched. That eliminates any DNA from both the driver and Carla. Further, the title to the truck had been recently issued out of Texas but was stolen from Florida. It makes me think this was not some DWI hit and run, but a planned hit." Joe looked at Sean and lifted his eyebrows, as if to say what about that.

Sean was not shocked by this news and fit what he believed happened—he just didn't know if it was Valenti or the Cartel. Sean felt he had to respond.

"I genuinely liked Carla. She was rough but seemed to have a good heart."

Joe couldn't resist a little smart-ass reply. "I am not sure your client Valenti has a heart. Seems like a ruthless son of a bitch.

"Something else I heard from the Kansas City FBI is that there seems to be a disagreement amongst the Valentis. Seems the brothers hold some resentment against their uncle taking the reins of the Family, and the uncle does not like the direction the brothers are heading."

Joe got very serious. "Do not let yourself get caught in the crossfire. I would not want to see you become a casualty."

Sean was taken aback by this revelation, and he knew that Joe was divulging more information than he probably had the authorization to provide.

Sean broke the tension. "Thanks for the heads-up. I will try to keep a low profile. Besides, I don't practice family law." Sean smiled, and Joe returned the smile.

Joe stood up to leave and extended his hand, which Sean shook with gratitude.

"Stay as long as you need with the files. I want you to know that I intend to move for a quick trial since we will have only one defendant. I will talk with the case manager and get back to you."

Sean took a deep breath after Joe closed the door and thought about the consequences of a Valenti feud. It could be that Uncle Augie was not on board with the close relationship John had developed with the San Miguel Cartel.

There was no telling the scope of the animosity between the uncle and his nephews. One thing was clear to Sean, not accepting a role with John Valenti was looking like the smartest decision he has made so far. Sean also knew that he had to discreetly pull information from John by carefully divulging what he had been told by the government. There was a narrow path he could travel with dangers from the government on one side and the mob on the other.

It was difficult for Sean to get John Valenti to the office. When John finally appeared, more than a week after Sean first contacted him, he looked haggard and ill at ease. Sean tried to ease into their conversation by talking about football and the games the past weekend. John cut him off and said that it had been a bad weekend for his coverage of bets on his sports book.

Sean then started reciting what he learned from the government reports. When Sean talked about the storage facilities in Houston, John's eyes lit up.

Sean asked, "Did you recognize something in what I said?"

John replied, "I am beginning to think that the rat might be from my end and not Mexico. I can't be certain yet. What else ya got for me?"

Sean told him about the fentanyl, the car exchange, and the meetings with San Miguel Cartel figures.

John said, "That could be anyone on either side of the border. The Mexicans will do their own house cleaning, but I need to be vigilant on my side. Anything else?"

Sean decided now was the time to broach the apparent conflict in the Kansas City family. "The prosecutor noted that there is a problem between you and your uncle. The feds are convinced that the Valenti family is in turmoil."

John became very angry. "What the fuck difference does that make? Do they have phone taps?"

Sean said, "There were no recordings or warrants in the material I reviewed. I guess my question to you is whether their information is true."

John relaxed slightly. "Yes, there are problems. My brother and I do not like some of the restrictions Uncle Augie has put in place. Because of this South Texas problem, he wants to cut off business with our partners in Mexico. Since that is where most of my income comes from, along with my brother, we are not happy. That is why I have been setting up shop here in Houston."

Sean took this opportunity to get John focused on how the

government got its information. "John, this is actually more information than the government should have been providing. I am sure that your quarrel with your uncle is not general knowledge in the Family, so who could be privy to that information and the border business interest. This is the person who will be testifying against you."

John nodded and said, "You are right, Sean. I am going to see what I can find out on a couple of our guys."

Sean added, "See if anyone had any unexplained absences. Whoever is cooperating is doing it to work off a case. So, most likely, it is someone with prior convictions that would be in serious trouble with a new case for cocaine or heroin."

John stood up to leave. "Let me put my mind to this issue and see what I discover."

Sean said, "Be careful, because if he is still working with you, he will probably be wired up. Although I think it is unlikely that the government would let him out of their grasp because they need him to make the case on you."

John shook his head to signify he understood. He exited Sean's office, picked up his cell phone from Sean's secretary, and left the office. Sean knew John's actions would either push the snitch to contact the government and go underground, or he would literally be put underground.

Chapter Ten
Change of Course

True to his word, the Assistant United States Attorney Joe Paggione was able to get Valenti's case set for a speedy trial—sixty days. Before there could be a jury trial, there was going to be a pretrial hearing to handle preliminary matters.

Valenti's case had been assigned to Federal District Judge Jon Weeks. Sean had dealt with Judge Weeks on numerous occasions and found him to be fair. In fact, Judge Weeks had a reputation as a 'tough judge on the government.' Unlike many of his brethren on the federal bench, he did not give the government the benefit of the doubt. As Judge Weeks stated many times in his courtroom, the government had all the money, people, and power compared to the average defendant, so they should be held to a strict standard. It was refreshing from a criminal defense lawyer's viewpoint, and Sean felt that it would benefit John Valenti.

Sean was dedicating much of his time to drafting a Motion to Suppress directed toward the papers seized from Valenti's wallet by the cop in South Texas. Other than the snitch's testimony, it was the only piece of evidence tying him to the San

Miguel Cartel. This was one of those times where this motion might make all the difference or no difference at all.

There was also a Memorandum of Law that would support the Motion to Suppress, which would cite to cases supporting the argument. The Anglo-American legal system was built upon prior court decisions providing the support for similar factual scenarios. These cases held particular value if they were based upon the United States Constitution and its amendments. The Fourth Amendment protection against unreasonable searches and seizures was especially relevant to Valenti's case.

However, no matter how persuasive the motion and any supporting memorandum were on paper, the key was to get the proper evidence from the investigating officers at the hearing. This was the stage where defense lawyers distinguished themselves or fell flat on their face. Sean hoped that he could be among the former group on Valenti's case.

As the date for pretrial hearing approached, Sean reached out to Valenti to meet with him. It was again difficult to get John Valenti to the office. He finally made an appearance a couple of days before the hearing. When Sean saw him, he had to comment on his appearance.

"You seem very happy… maybe a new woman in your life?"

"Hardly. I think that I may have an answer to the snitch problem." Valenti seemed smug about it.

Sean asked, "You mean you have figured out who it is?"

"Exactly. It is a guy who acted as the coordinator of the dope pickup from the Mexicans and seeing that my people knew what vehicle to pick up. He was paid commissions by both the cartel and me. His health was in question before this whole snitch theory because he had been double-dipping and self-dealing."

Sean said, "This provides background for what he can testify about. Does he have much personal knowledge about you and your connection to the dope pickups?"

Valenti nodded assent. "The final touch is that he can't be found now. He has not even showed to pick up his last payment."

Valenti smiled and added, "We have some access to information from the feds. I anticipate that the snitch will be located before too long,"

Sean knew that this did not bode well for the government's witness.

"I have to put this out there, John. If you are involved in killing a government witness, you could be looking at a capital murder charge. Death penalty."

Valenti appeared unfazed. "I am not going to be doing anything. My friends and associates are looking out for me.

"There is something else happening. My brother and I are consolidating our resources from Kansas City to Houston. I will be putting all my energy into Texas operations."

Sean was not sure that he liked John Valenti making Houston his base of operations. There was not much he could do about it, though. He decided that he should get Valenti focused on the upcoming hearing.

"Next Tuesday we will be litigating the motion to suppress the paper with the contact phone numbers. If we are successful, then any independent connections to the cartel members will be prohibited from use at trial. Of course, the government still has the informant, but any confirmation of his testimony by that paper would be gone."

Valenti smiled and said, "That paper may be all the government will have."

Sean continued, "Anyway, you may have to testify at the hearing if the cop decides to change the story. You would only testify regarding the stop and the search, and no other testimony would be allowed."

Valenti nodded and said, "I am not happy about it, but I will do what has to be done."

Sean said, "Let's review what happened again."

John Valenti narrated his driving to the Valley, meeting with the cartel contact, and then being stopped by the Texas trooper. He reaffirmed that he had no weapons on him at the time (at least on his person) and no narcotics. The only evidence was the phone numbers of the cartel members.

After reviewing these scenarios numerous times with Valenti, Sean thanked him and said he would see him on Tuesday morning in Judge Week's courtroom.

Tuesday morning Sean appeared in Judge Weeks courtroom by 9:30 A.M. He always tried to be early to get settled and comfortable with the courtroom. This federal courtroom, like most he had been privy to, was cavernous—with twenty-foot ceilings and granite backdrops behind the imposing bench for the judge. Sean knew that it was intentionally out of scale to portray the power that the federal judge wields. No one could be in this courtroom and not feel intimidated. It was the duty of the defense lawyer to move past that so he or she could be an effective advocate for his/her client.

While Sean was sitting at the table assigned to defense counsel, Assistant United States Attorney Joe Paggione marched in. A couple of federal agents trailed in his wake. When Sean looked up, he could see that Paggione was upset.

"What did your client do with our witness?"

Sean did not have to feign surprise. He softly said, "Pardon me. I really don't know what you are talking about."

Paggione sat down opposite Sean and glared at him. "Our witness has disappeared and you can imagine, we suspect the worst."

As if on cue, John Valenti entered the courtroom. Paggione shot him a vicious look.

Sean broke the silence. "What evidence do you have that would lead you to accuse Mr. Valenti? Why not the cartel members? Besides, if your witness was in federal custody, how could anyone get to him?"

Paggione looked at the floor. "That is still being looked at. Suffice to say it appears that my witness was picked up while tying loose ends before his extended time in protective custody. I will present more to the Court."

Paggione stood up and went over to the government's table with the federal agents. Sean got up and motioned for Valenti to go out into the hall. When they were outside the courtroom and away from listening ears, Sean spoke to Valenti.

"The government claims their witness is gone and they are insinuating you are involved. Is there any likelihood that they could prove that?"

Valenti bowed his head and replied, "I personally had nothing to do with anything other than suggesting to some business associates my suspicions on who the snitch might be. It appears I was correct." With that, Valenti raised his head and smiled.

Sean replied, "Don't look smug, and for God's sake, do not let anyone in the court, and in particular, the judge, have any notion that you figured out the informant. Let's go back in and sit in the audience until I tell you to come to the defense table."

Sean and Valenti entered the courtroom together, and Sean went back to his table. A few minutes later, the familiar knocking sounded announcing the arrival of the judge.

When the judge was seated, the federal prosecutor Paggione said, "Your Honor, may we approach the bench for a conference?"

Judge Weeks motioned for the lawyers to come up. In federal court, the bench area was raised high so that the lawyers had to go up a couple steps to come to the side of the bench to talk to the judge. Judge Weeks motioned for the clerks to shut off the microphones, which were usually on the entire time a hearing or trial was occurring. Paggione took the lead since he asked for the conference.

"Your Honor, the government has encountered a problem with the case against John Valenti. The cooperating witness has disappeared. The government suspects that Mr. Valenti is involved."

Judge Weeks stared at Paggione and said, "What do you expect the Court to do about that?"

Paggione looked uncomfortable and shifted his weight from foot to foot.

"The government felt an obligation to inform the Court as to the status in that we may seek a continuance on the trial."

Judge Weeks frowned and said in a menacing voice, "The incompetence of the government to protect its witnesses is not in the province of this Court. Without specific evidence that Mr. Valenti caused this disappearance, there is nothing for the Court to do. You do not have evidence of Mr. Valenti's role, do you?"

Paggione shook his head to signify no. The judge continued, "Does it effect this motion hearing today?" Both Sean and Paggione replied negatively. "Well then, let's get on with the business of this Court."

Judge Weeks signified that the conference was over and both Sean and Paggione returned to their seats. Sean stood and informed the judge that the items were seized from John Valenti without a warrant and therefore required to be justified by the government. When Sean sat down, Joe Paggione stood and called Texas Department of Public Safety Trooper Daniel Hill. Trooper Hill walked to the witness stand with his cowboy hat under one arm. After being sworn by the clerk, he took his seat.

Paggione began, "Please state your full name and your occupation."

"Daniel Hill. I am a peace officer employed by the Texas Department of Public Safety."

"How long have you been an officer with DPS?"

"I was a police officer in the McAllen Police Department for almost ten years, then I transferred to be a Trooper for the Texas Department of Public Safety."

"Officer Hill, do you have experience in handling narcotics cases?'

"Yes. Anyone who is in law enforcement in the Rio Grande Valley will have some experience with narcotics cases due to the huge volume moving across the border."

Paggione next pulled up two mugshots on his computer which were then broadcast to the multiple monitors in the courtroom.

"Officer Hill, do you recognize these men?"

Officer Hill dutifully looked at the screen in front of him in the witness box.

"Yes, they are members of the San Miguel Cartel. The man on the left is Saul Carrera, commonly known as Snake Eyes. I believe the other man is Pedro Soliz."

Paggione said, "Are these men involved with narcotics?"

Officer Hill took on a serious demeanor. "Carrera, the man known as Snake Eyes, is the reputed head of the San Miguel Cartel and is involved with moving huge quantities of marijuana, cocaine, heroin and lately, fentanyl. Pedro Soliz is his lieutenant and enforcer. In my years of investigating and arresting individuals in the drug trade, the San Miguel Cartel stands out as the largest and most ruthless drug group along the border."

Paggione continued questioning. "Let's go back to May 10th of last year. Did you have an opportunity to come into contact with the defendant John Valenti?"

"Yes sir, I did."

"What were the circumstances that brought you into contact with Mr. Valenti?"

Officer Hill was quiet for a moment, then said, "I was contacted by an Agent Harris of the DEA, who told me that

Mr. Valenti was coming into town to meet with some San Miguel Cartel members."

Sean abruptly stood up. "Objection. Hearsay."

Judge Weeks said, "I will allow it solely to understand the state of mind of the witness. Continue."

Paggione asked, "Were you requested to do anything?"

"Agent Harris asked me to keep an eye out for him and he gave me the hotel he was staying at while in McAllen."

Paggione asked, "Did you have any information that provided a reason to infer that Mr. Valenti was involved in criminal activity?"

Officer Hill stated, "I knew that John Valenti was a member of a crime family from Kansas City and combined with the information from the DEA that he was meeting with the San Miguel Cartel leaders, it was a knowledgeable deduction that he was here on criminal business."

Paggione continued, "How did you specifically come into contact with Mr. Valenti?"

Officer Hill serenely replied, "I witnessed a traffic violation and so I took this as an opportunity to see what he was doing in town."

Paggione looked flustered. "Was this something that you worked out with the DEA ahead of time?"

"No. I felt that it was necessary for me to ascertain what a mobster is doing in my town."

Paggione continued but looked concerned.

"Did you find anything illegal on Mr. Valenti?"

"No. I did not."

"What did you find?"

"I found a paper that had phone numbers that subsequent investigation showed were attached to some cartel members. Saul Carrera, in particular."

Officer Hill appeared proud of his accomplishment.

Paggione's showed a picture of a paper with two phone members, and one had initials "S.C" next to the number.

"Officer Hill, is this the paper you retrieved from Mr. Valenti?"

"Yes sir, it is."

Paggione stood and said, "Pass the witness your Honor."

As Sean stood to start his cross exam of the officer, Judge Weeks turned to the witness and said, "Where did you retrieve this paper?"

The trooper appeared shaken being addressed by the federal judge, but he replied, "I took the paper from Mr. Valenti's wallet."

The judge sat back and was obviously bothered by this answer. Sean requested permission to proceed and Judge Weeks assented.

"Now Officer Hill, you did not have any independent probable cause of wrongdoing by Mr. Valenti, did you?"

Officer Hill stoically said, "No, I did not."

"You were solely acting out of your need to discover what was going on with John Valenti in your town?"

"It was my reasoned judgment that Mr. Valenti was in McAllen to conduct criminal business."

Sean shot back, "You do realize that stopping and searching citizens, no matter their affiliation, requires probable cause?"

"That may ordinarily be true, but this was an exceptional

situation involving leaders in large criminal organizations."

Sean saw his opportunity. "Do you agree that the U.S. Constitution confers standards that apply to all regardless of perceived affiliations?"

Officer Hill looked down then said, "I believe that is true, but this opportunity required actions."

Sean stated, "Even if no probable cause existed?"

Officer Hill stated, "Yes."

Sean realized that nothing further need be asked. "Pass the witness."

Judge Weeks now took control. "You can both save your arguments for another day. First, I would like to commend Officer Hill for being forthright and honest. It was refreshing. However, the educated assumption of an experienced police officer still does not rise to the level of proximate cause. Moreover, I do not see any evidence of reason for the traffic stop, which also would not support the search of Mr. Valenti's wallet. This paper will not be allowed at Mr. Valenti's trial and is hereby suppressed.

"Mr. Paggione, please keep the Court informed as to the likelihood of the trial and the status of your witness."

Judge Weeks stood up and walked into his chambers.

John Valenti shook Sean's hand and gloated. "This calls for a celebration. How about dinner at Tony's?"

Sean said, "Okay. You get the reservation and I am there." He then went over to Paggione.

"Do let me know if the witness appears and whether we will be going to trial."

Paggone looked crestfallen. "It will be impossible without

the witness. I need to review with my superiors and will let you know."

It was with a great feeling of relief that Sean packed up and left the courtroom. As he walked to the elevator, John Valenti was conversing with a couple of men, but stopped to yell at Sean, "Seven thirty at Tony's. See you there."

Sean arrived at Tony's promptly at 7:30 P.M. He gave his Corvette to the valet, put on his sports coat and entered the rarefied air of this bastion of upper-class dining. Tony's was well-known as the place to see and be seen on the dining circuit and had been for a considerable time period.

When he approached the hostess and gave Valenti's name, he was escorted to a table just outside the main dining area, so that there was some privacy. Sean noted that the table was for four and that he was the first to arrive. A bottle of Dom Perignon was chilling in an ice bucket. The sommelier came by, opened the bottle, and poured a glass, he said, "Your host specifically requested that I open the bottle and pour a glass for you. Enjoy."

Sean never turned down a glass of vintage bubbly, and immediately took a mouthful of the fine champagne. Although the table was not centered, it did provide good viewing of the society dames and rich oil men dropping by other tables to socialize.

Sean recognized many of the women from the society pages of the Houston Chronicle. Some had faces so taut that smiling was difficult, but others had been surgically enhanced so well guessing their age was impossible. Sean thoroughly enjoyed the show, until John Valenti came striding through. He was alone.

When he arrived, Sean asked, "Will we be dining with anyone else?"

John sat down, grabbed the champagne bottle, and poured a glass. "I thought my brother might join us, but he headed back to Kansas City. Anyway, salud on a job well done."

Valenti lifted his glass and Sean followed suit.

Sean said, "I wish I could take credit for great lawyering, but our best witness was an honest cop."

Valenti laughed and said, "It takes a good lawyer to know when to let the facts play out, and you are that lawyer."

The waiter showed up at the table with huge one-page menus with all the items offered in calligraphy. Tony's was an Italian restaurant with a Continental twist. Sean selected prosciutto ham and honeydew melon to start, and a rare tuna steak for the main course. Valenti went more traditional Italian with a Caprese salad and prawns with fettucine Alfredo. When the waiter left, Valenti leaned in to the table with Sean in a hushed tone.

"As I told you before, I am taking my business from KC to Houston. I am keeping my ties to Laredo but I am no longer going to visit there. I think I am 'persona non grata,' and truth be told, I was never fond of the place anyway." Valenti smiled, sipped his champagne, and continued.

"I want to keep you on a retainer to represent my interests. I know that you do not want to be a counselor, but I want to ensure your status as my lawyer first, and anyone working for me next."

Sean said, "John, I don't want a retainer because that could make me part of the organization. It would expose me to criminal prosecution. I also do not want to be privy to your future illegal activities. All the information I need will be when criminal prosecution may be imminent or an arrest has occurred. I will be your lawyer whenever you need me to protect you or your interests. I just don't want to be part of the group."

Valenti shook his head. "Understood, Counselor. You should know that my brother is trying to consolidate his position in Kansas City so that we can join forces."

At this point the waiter arrived with the salad and the melon. As he poured champagne, he noted the bottle was getting light. Valenti ordered another bottle of Dom Perignon.

As soon as the waiter left, Valenti said, "I believe that the government's case will go away. I do not believe they will have a witness." With that, Valenti again raised his glass.

Sean realized that no response was his best option as way of reply. It was not unforeseen anyway.

As the first course was cleared and the entrees delivered, Sean and Valenti made small talk about sports and the weather.

After the meal, as the second bottle of Dom was disappearing, Valenti did mention that he was going to open a strip club in town. He casually mentioned that such clubs were great places to 'wash money.' Sean realized that it was the champagne talking, but Valenti was obviously kicking things into gear in Texas.

Chapter Eleven
New Business

True to his word, John Valenti was kicking his enterprises into gear. Sean could tell because he started getting referrals on unlikely cases outside of his usual criminal clients. There were a couple women from a high-end call girl business charged with prostitution. There was a bookie charged with gambling and organized criminal activity. Finally, there was an older Hispanic man charged with transporting heroin across the Laredo bridge from Mexico.

Each of these clients came to Sean's office clutching his card. Although never stingy with giving out his card, Sean could not remember putting out a large number of cards to anyone recently, except John Valenti, who had specifically requested the cards and sent someone to pick them up. Sean was not going to complain, since each client paid the fee quoted.

Each of these cases, except the heroin smuggling case, were being resolved without much hassle. The 'working girls' had their cases reduced to low end misdemeanors and paid a fine. The bookie had the organized criminal activity dismissed and pled to a misdemeanor with payment of the maximum fine of

$2,000. Victimless crimes often were resolved for fines since money made the system work.

The heroin case was another matter. The driver of a pickup transporting produce from Mexico, had ten kilos of heroin hidden in watermelons. The dogs alerted to the drugs, even inside the melons. The driver was Carlos Reyna and he had a produce distribution business in Laredo. Charges were brought in Laredo Federal Court and Sean appeared for the initial appearance. Due to the amount of heroin involved a bond was denied. Carlos was disappointed, but not surprised.

What was surprising to Sean was the revelation by Carlos that he did not work for the cartel but had a recent investor from Houston financing his activities. Carlos noted that he only recently got into the smuggling aspect but had been getting produce from Mexico for years. Business had been rough lately and the financial angel had saved him. Carlos did not reveal the name and Sean did not press it.

While this new business was being handled, Sean was looking to resolve some of the other outstanding issues involving Valenti.

First, Sean needed to ascertain what had happened with the grand jury investigation in Dallas with Cicero's men. An investigation with the federal district clerk's office determined that the grand jury term had expired. Although federal indictments could be issued with no trace for a lawyer to find until the client got arrested, it was not the usual course. Sean contacted the Assistant United States attorneys he dealt with, who said that no further grand jury action was planned. As far as Sean was concerned, that meant that the case was dead. Sean had his secretary contact Mr. Green (the anonymous connection for Lou Cicero) to relay the good news.

Next on the agenda was finding out what was happening on the Dragon Imports case in San Diego with Peter Suh. Sean has a few long conversations with the San Diego lawyer, Paul Grant, who relayed that the United States Attorney's office was shifting its attention to the pharmaceutical distributors. Since Dragon Imports had the FDA license to distribute the fentanyl, the government decided to focus on the local distributor and its relationship to the San Miguel Cartel. Grant told Sean that he anticipated a dismissal predicated on the cooperation of Suh to trace the chain of custody to the San Diego distributor.

Finally, since the trial date was approaching on Valenti's case, Sean reached out to the prosecutor Joe Paggione for a status. Paggione admitted that the witness had disappeared and that he was forced to file a dismissal without prejudice. This meant that the government could refile charges against John Valenti if the witness surfaced, which Sean felt was highly unlikely.

Sean set up a meeting with Valenti for a week afterward due to Valenti being out of town again. After getting this series of good news, Sean went to see Janey at Foxes. While he was enjoying her company, and arranging a celebratory dinner together, Sean's former Northside client stopped by his table. Janey excused herself and Mando slid in beside Sean.

"I was hoping I might find you here. Do you have your phone on you?"

Sean pulled his phone out and Mando motioned to a tough-looking tattooed man nearby. Both Sean and Mando gave their phones to the guy and Mando told him in Spanish to find a far-away corner. Sean spoke enough Spanish to understand, if not to speak fluently.

After the guy left with the phone, Mando turned to Sean.

"Your client, John Valenti, is making it hard on the street business on the Northside. He has a group of new dealers he has recruited to sell heroin, coke, meth, and weed. The quality is good and he is keeping prices low. He is making it difficult for a hard-working pachuco like myself to make a living." Mando smiled as he said this.

"He is also pumping the heroin, coke, and meth with that fentanyl shit. He cuts the drugs down and adds a little of the fentanyl to make it seem stronger. There is a problem is that shit is killing people way more than the real shit. This is bringing more heat on the streets."

Sean looked at Mando. "Why are you telling me this? I do not control him, and, as you know, I stay out of everyone's business."

Mando leaned in and looked at Sean with narrowed hard eyes.

"Word on the street in that you are a counselor for his family here."

This revelation shook Sean. He sat back speechless at first. Finally, he said, "That is not true. I am Valenti's lawyer and represent some of his associates. Nothing more than being a criminal defense lawyer."

Mando nodded his head. "I believe that, but word on the street has its own life. You might tell that pendejo to leave some of the customers alive."

Mando got up from the booth and retrieved Sean's phone. As Mando left, he said, "Watch yourself. Things may get ugly."

Sean sat in the booth and nursed his scotch. Janey came back over and Sean put on his best smile.

"Why don't you go get dressed and we will go for a nice dinner."

Two days later, Sean was driving with Janey down to Laredo. It was about a five-hour drive from Houston but was easy interstate highway all the way. Sean set the Corvette on eighty most of the way but liked to kick it above one hundred when the open spaces of Texas allowed.

Sean was going to Laredo to meet again with his client and get discovery on the case from the government. Janey came along to shop in the Laredo stores which had items carried in the Houston stores for a fraction of the cost. It was because Laredo was the main point of entry from Mexico and many of the clothes went through there, at least that was Sean's best guess. It kept Janey happy while he dealt with the legal matters.

Their residence was the best hotel in town, La Posada. It was Spanish architecture with tile floors, stucco walls, and heavy wooden beams in the ceiling. It was like being in old Mexico. It used to be customary for Texans to cross the bridge to Nuevo Laredo, Mexico for the dog races, the bordellos of Boys Town, or the famous Cadillac Bar. That changed when the cartels took control of the border. Now Laredo was the end of the line.

The next morning Sean walked to the federal courthouse

and was provided the government's file. It had no revelations other than the purity of the heroin: less than fifty percent.

After reviewing the file, Sean met with the prosecutor Jesse Gomez. He made the standard government offer for cooperation in return for leniency in the sentencing. Federal cases were based on guidelines that determined what a sentence should be. Due to the amount of heroin, Carlos was looking at a mandatory minimum of twenty years. Since there was little to be done on challenging the search, Carlos would need some help.

Sean told the prosecutor, "I will talk with him about cooperating, but you know how the cartels operate. He would be jeopardizing his family, and himself. One thing that bothers me about this seizure, the quality of the heroin is far below the purity of street heroin in Houston."

Jesse said, "I noticed that. It has been happening often now. We almost never saw anything below ninety percent. The purity levels changed a couple years ago."

It was apparent to both attorneys that the smugglers were cutting the heroin to maximize profits and then add fentanyl on the distributor side.

Sean told the prosecutor, Jesse, that he would get back to him. Sean then returned to the hotel, retrieved his Corvette and drove out to the federal detention facility. There Sean explained the situation to his client, Carlos. Carlos was not inclined to provide any information, but knew he had to make a deal. Sean explained that often people like Carlos may have worked with were now dead. This could be cooperation without much risk since the government can't go after a dead man. There was no need to decide now, but Sean let his suggestion hang there. Sean did mention the low purity and Carlos feigned ignorance. As Carlos explained it, "Not my problem."

Sean returned to Laredo and the La Posada hotel. When he arrived at the room, Janey had numerous bags and boxes. She proudly showed Sean the many dresses, shoes, and undies she had purchased. It always humored Sean that women took such pride in their shopping 'skills.' It seemed analogous to a fisherman showing his prize catch, and that was something Sean could identify with.

After reviewing all her items, Sean said, "Pick out a nice new dress and shoes, because we are going to the best restaurant in town. It is called the Tack Room." As Sean turned to go take a shower, he gestured at all the boxes and bags. "You do realize that we are driving a Corvette and storage is not one of it attributes."

Janey gave one of her best smiles and said, "I am sure you will figure a way to make it fit. I will make it worth your effort."

Sean realized he couldn't argue with that.

The Tack Room was in a building constructed in the 1880s, and like the name implied, was decorated with all things related to horses and horse racing. The restaurant had heavy wood beams in the ceiling and wooden booths with green leather seating. The atmosphere was old money and the cuisine revolved around steaks. It was located contiguous to La Posada, so no driving was required.

After getting situated in one of the booths, Sean and Janey ordered cocktails, then a bottle of Simi Cabernet to accompany their steaks. After the waiter opened the cabernet, three men approached the table. They were all wearing heavy gold neck-laces and exotic skin cowboy boots. One of the men stepped forward and placed a velvet Crown Royal bag on the table. This man had piercing, dark eyes and an engaging smile.

As he placed the bag on the table, he said, "Counselor, la propina por su trabajo por mi amigos."

Sean smiled back and said, "No es necessario."

The man stopped smiling and said again, "La propina. Comprende."

Sean realized he needed to show gratitude, not an unwillingness to accept this gift. "Gracias Señor."

With that, the man smiled again and stepped back to leave but managed one last comment. "Muy bonita mujer. Buenas noches."

Sean mumbled again. "Gracias. Buenas noches." Sean then noticed as the man turned to go that he wore rattlesnake boots, it was also obvious that the other men were his bodyguards.

Janey turned to Sean and said, "What was that about?"

Sean looked at her. "We have just had a visit from the head of the San Miguel Cartel. He is known as 'Snake Eyes' and is one of the most wanted men in North America. He basically paid me a tip, called 'propina,' for my past services. I guess?" With that, Sean opened the velvet bag to find three stacks of one hundred dollar bills with a wrapper on each noting "Ten Thousand Dollars."

Sean smiled and said, "Yeah, it is quite a nice tip. He also paid you a compliment as he left, calling you a very pretty woman."

Janey looked bewildered. "Does this happen very often?"

Sean said, "I can't remember receiving a tip before. But it would have been not in our best interest to refuse. On the bright side, why don't we see whether the restaurant has any old Bordeaux in its cellar?"

Sean figured he might as well make a good night of it with his new found winnings. As Sean perused the old Bordeaux listings, he had a nagging feeling bothering him. How did 'Snake Eyes' know where he was? How much more did he know about Sean and his ties to Valenti? Finally, why give Sean money and profess it to be a tip? Maybe Valenti could answer these questions, but for now Sean was going to have a good time with his pretty woman.

John Valenti finally came in to see Sean the week after he returned from Laredo. He set the meeting late in the afternoon so that there would be no conflicts in Sean's schedule, and also to drink whiskey.

After putting the cell phones in Maria's lead box, they each grabbed a scotch and some ice from the bar in the office. Sean had always liked the look of a bar in a private law office. Sean had worked out many cases sipping whiskey. It was widely known to both state and federal prosecutors that they could negotiate and drink at Sean's office. It helped resolve many difficult cases.

As Sean and Valenti sat down, Sean got up and went to the door of his office. He leaned out and told Maria to go home. This meeting might last a while and Sean wanted no interruption.

Sean started the conversation. "All seems to be going well

on your legal fronts. First, the government has filed a dismissal on your indictment. You will be surprised to know that the witness against you cannot be located." This made John Valenti smile.

"Further, the case against Peter Suh and Dragon Imports appears to be going away. The government is going to change their focus to the San Diego recipient of the fentanyl.

"Finally, the investigation on the stolen cars and Texas titles does not have traction. The government was looking for one of the Miami boys to crack and that ain't happening."

Sean took a sip of his whiskey and then continued. "There is a produce distributor in Laredo who I currently represent and who you may know. His name is Carlos Reyna and he was caught bringing low-grade heroin across the border."

Valenti said, "What do you mean by 'low-grade' heroin?"

Sean answered, "It was about fifty percent pure, which is way below street potency in Houston. The only way that could be commercially viable is to up the potency by adding something to make it stronger, such as fentanyl."

Valenti said, "Seems reasonable. Why tell me?"

"I was visited by a former client from the Northside of Houston and he tells me your people are putting the fentanyl on the street."

Valenti answered belligerently, "How does this asshole know it's related to me? Why is he telling you?"

Sean replied, "He told me because word on the street is that I am your counselor on your business. I set him straight but word on the street has a life of its own."

Valenti leaned back in the chair and took a long drink of his whiskey. After a prolonged silence, Valenti started talking.

"I have been getting into many ventures in this city. I am trying to spread my wings and see what I can fly into. I believe you may be representing a few of my employees.

"I know that you do not want the specifics of any enterprises, but I want you aware it is going on so you can be ready to defend me."

Sean nodded affirmatively and let Valenti keep talking.

"Basically, I have put together a family organization in Houston with a principal outreach to the Valley and the Border.

"This city has many ethnic organizations but no one trying to tie them together. That is where I am going with this concept. Sort of like a *Lord of the Rings,* with one ring to rule the other rings of power. I get to wear the one ring."

Sean had not noticed that John Valenti was becoming so self-important and power hungry. These were dangerous personality flaws in the criminal world. Sean felt he had to bring some hard reality into this discussion.

"Don't you think that the Nigerians or the Pakistanis or the Vietnamese might take offense with your power grab?"

Valenti smiled and said, "That is my plan. I did not say it was in effect yet."

"I met 'Snake Eyes' while I was having dinner in Laredo. He gave me a tip of $30,000. Do you know about this?"

Valenti laughed. "I told him that the problem on the border went away because of your work. I did not think he would reward you. Well, good for you."

Sean asked, "Do you know how he knew where to find me?"

Valenti got serious. "You are in his backyard. He knows who comes in and is involved in anything in which he has an interest. The cartel boys also have geeks that can trace anyone's cell phone. Finding you was no big deal."

Sean didn't know whether he should be relieved or more worried.

Valenti now changed topics. "I have some other matters that concern me. It is not that I want you to advise me but I feel like you should know what is happening with the Family in Kansas City. My brother and I are trying to remove my uncle as the Family head. He is an obstruction to the plans in Texas, and frankly, he wants me to curtail all the business I have set up here."

Valenti flashed anger and took a minute to cool down. Sean sat quietly to let him continue.

"So my brother David is setting up the move against my uncle Augie. He has been meeting with the members and the general feeling is with us. David would stay in KC and I would handle Texas, but we would work together."

Sean knew that both John and David Valenti were aware that what they were doing was tantamount to treason. Death was the usual punishment for treason. John Valenti took a long drink of his scotch and continued his narrative.

"I have also started using bodyguards, which I had avoided in the past. Always thought it brought too much attention. However, Lou Cicero has done it forever and he still flies under the Fed's radar. In fact, it was Snake Eyes and his captain who convinced me to get protection.

"The San Miguel Cartel is worried because my uncle has

made overtures to their main competitors on the border. Uncle Augie wants to have a line on a drug supply other than through me. The San Miguel boys want me healthy to continue our business venture, and they sense some coming danger."

Valenti drained his glass. "What you have related is good news. We need to keep the government at bay so that my ventures can go forward."

Valenti got up to go out the office door and Sean rose to open the door. When they went into main area, all the secretaries and staff were gone but two large men were sitting in the reception area. Valenti shook Sean's hand and left with a guy in front and one in back.

Sean thought John Valenti was looking like a mob boss already, and his actions would ensure that he was one. *The reward better be worth the risk,* thought Sean, *but whatever occurs, I need to be distanced from whatever actions John and David Valenti take against their uncle. Some blood is sure to be spilled.*

Chapter Twelve
Crisis Management

A few weeks after meeting with John Valenti, Sean was getting ready to go to court. He usually played jazz CDs while he showered, shaved, and dressed. This morning he put on the morning news.

The woman newscaster caught his ear with her broadcast. "This just into our newsroom from Kansas City. The son of deceased alleged mob boss Gus Valenti was shot and killed yesterday. David Valenti was cutting his grass on a riding lawnmower when he was shot with what police are calling a high caliber rifle. David Valenti was known to authorities as a member of the Valenti Crime Family in Kansas City. His uncle Augie Valenti is reputed to be the current boss of the crime family. David Valenti leaves behind two children and a wife. No word on possible suspects by the authorities."

Sean was taken aback by the story. He immediately started thinking back to his conversation with John Valenti. The shooting of David had to be retribution by the uncle, but there might be other parties who were testing the Valenti Family. Sean tried to call John Valenti, but Sean only received a message that the number was unavailable. That seemed odd, but Sean had business he needed to attend to at the courthouse, so he dressed and drove into downtown Houston.

After handling the case duties at the courthouse, Sean returned to his office. He asked Maria if she had heard from John Valenti, and she replied negatively. Maria remarked on the news story about David Valenti and asked if there were any danger to John Valenti. Sean told her that he had no information to determine what was going on. Sean went into his office and closed the door. He thought about calling a number he had for John in Kansas City, but knew it was a central 'Valenti Family' line. That did not seem like a prudent course of action.

Sean also thought about calling Paggione, the federal prosecutor, but he would most likely be in the dark at this stage. Better to wait a couple days and see what develops, thought Sean.

After Maria and the other people in the office left at five. Sean stayed to get more work done. About seven, he heard the door to the reception area open. He called out, "Who is there?"

When there was no immediate reply, Sean exited his office into the reception area. There was John Valenti with his bodyguards. Valenti looked relieved to see Sean. He told his men to wait in the reception seating area, and he followed Sean toward his office. When Sean asked for Valenti's phone, he shrugged his shoulder and said, "Don't have one." Sean put his in the lead box and they went into his office and closed the door.

Valenti headed over to the bar and poured a whiskey. He then sat down in the client chair across from Sean's desk. Sean decided to let Valenti start the conversation. Valenti was sipping his whiskey and looking into the glass.

Finally, he broke the silence. "I know you probably heard about David's murder. That is courtesy of my uncle Augie.

"I admit that David and I were testing the limits of the Family rules, but killing David was unnecessary. We could have separated ways and continued to go forward.

"Uncle Augie saw this setup in Houston as a direct challenge to his authority. He did not appreciate the close relationship that I developed with the San Miguel Cartel. I was specifically warned by some of the members that he was trying to freeze me out of their business. When Snake Eyes refused to go along, Uncle Augie went to a competing cartel, the Alphas. This caused bad blood all around."

John stopped and took a sip of his whiskey. Sean had known that there was some challenge to Augie's authority by John, but it was now apparent that Augie was trying to eliminate his nephews.

John continued, "Augie was intent on David using his contacts with the Alphas to get his drugs. David continued to come through me.

"I will be honest with you. We knew this was a slap in Uncle Augie's face, but we thought that a deal could be reached. David also felt like he could get the backing of the family capos and appeal to their ability to earn more with our contacts." John hesitated and sipped his whiskey again, which gave Sean an opening to interject.

"John, are you telling me that neither you nor David made a move to take your Uncle Augie out of the picture altogether?"

John stared into his glass. "David had reached out to an independent who did work for the cartels. We did not want our fingerprints on anything that would directly tie us to Augie's death. David and I gave him a deposit and he was going to research how to do it and get back to us. That was a couple days ago."

John dropped his head down and quietly said, "Looks like he flipped on us or he did the set up to take out my brother. We were careless and trusted the wrong people." John started quietly sobbing.

Sean reached behind his desk and handed a box of tissues to John. He took one and wiped his eyes.

Sean asked, "Do you have specific information that Augie is coming after you?"

John replied, "Nothing specific. It seems only logical that he would want a clean slate."

Sean said, "Not necessarily. Maybe you can reach out through some of your contacts, like Lou Cicero or Pesce in New Orleans. None of them like to see blood feuds in the families."

John said, "That is an idea. I have basically hunkered down. I suppose that is where I turn next."

John stood up to leave and Sean said, "Hold on. Let me get some things together and I will go down with you."

While Sean was getting his brief case and turning off the lights, Valenti told one of the bodyguards to go get his car. Sean locked the main doors. Valenti, his second guard, and Sean went down in the elevator. They crossed the large stone lobby to glass doors that led to a circular drive and a parking structure attached to his building. Sean told Valenti to keep him apprised of any funeral for his brother. Valenti agreed and walked down the drive to his car.

Sean continued into the parking garage to some open stairs that went to the second level where the Corvette was parked. As Sean started up the stairs, he saw a vehicle driving down the first level at a fast pace. At that some moment, he heard the distinctive pop of a handgun and the staccato of an automatic weapon. Sean was at the top of the stairs at the second level and he instinctively dove next to the large SUV parked by the stairs. Bullets started shattering glass, ricocheting off the concrete, and hitting the metal of nearly cars with a thud.

Sean was shaken but realized he had to get somewhere else. Fast. He knew he was a sitting duck in this parking structure. He managed to look around as the black Escalade drove ahead on the first level. Sean realized immediately that the vehicle would have to exit, swing around the service drive and come back in to get to the second floor. This was his chance.

Sean knew that below the first level of parking there was another level and it had access to outside. Sean crawled over to the opening on the second level and dropped down to the first level. He then did the same to get to the bottom level. He realized that the support pillars acted as a screen between him and his assassins. He heard the squealing of tires as the Escalade went up to the second level, just as he got on the bottom level.

The bottom level had an opening that cut along the length of the parking garage, but exited to grass, not concrete. Sean ran over to the opening and pulled himself out and on to the grass outside. Immediately behind the parking garage was a large apartment complex. Sean started running towards the buildings that would shield him from the parking garage. Once he was on the side of the apartment building away from the garage, he sat down behind some bushes to settle down and think. *Who the hell would want me dead? Was John Valenti already dead? Did Augie Valenti try to kill me as well?*

While sitting on the ground, Sean realized that his left arm hurt and then noticed blood on his hand. He still had his suit coat, so he tried to take it off but it hurt too much to try. Since the coat was dark blue, any blood was not readily apparent. He did take off his tie and put it in his pocket for possible use later as a tourniquet.

Sean suddenly realized that he had a honing beacon for the killers. He had to assume that these men could trace his cell phone. Before he got rid of it, he had to think of how he might use it first.

He could not go back to his car. There was probably one guy sitting on that right now. He could not go home because they would go there next. An Uber was risky, but possible. He needed a "port in the storm" and then he thought of Janey. No way could he go to the bar where she worked. He could walk to her Montrose bungalow which was about two miles away.

Now he just had to reach her. A call was risky because they might follow it to the source. His best idea was to send a text, which was more difficult to trace. He did not know the extent of the resources available to these men but he had to figure that they had mafia and maybe cartel backing. Either would not stop until he was dead.

Sean pulled up Janey's phone number and sent a text. "Meet me at the Bungalow. I need your help. ASAP."

Sean had to get rid of the cell phone. He turned the phone off and took off the protective case. Then Sean beat the phone against the back of the building to open the back. This gave him access to the SIM card.

Sean stood up and started walking. He realized that he was unsteady at first but the adrenaline would keep him going. He threw the SIM card in a nearby sewer grate and realized all his contacts and pictures were now gone. As he walked along the street, he found a pickup truck and threw the phone into the bed of the truck under the toolbox attached to the bed of the truck. Hopefully, this would confuse any would-be trackers.

As Sean walked along, he noticed that he looked ragged. His pants were torn at the knee, and he had a blood-soaked jacket. The saving grace was that he was walking into the Montrose area where addicts, whores, homeless people, and numerous party goers were located. He might just fit in.

It was also late fall, almost Halloween, and the weather was temperate. He could walk along with his suit coat on and not appear too conspicuous. Montrose is an older area of Houston comprised of a warren of streets with a variety of residential structures, bars, and shops.

Sean walked out of the apartment complex and crossed a major road. His first instinct was to get into the back streets. He found one of the residential streets that ran far into Montrose. After what seemed a long walk, Sean came into an area he recognized with a series of bars. Many of these places had outside seating areas and many people hanging out. His best hope was to blend with the masses.

As Sean walked along the bar scene on lower Westheimer, he saw a black Cadillac Escalade moving along in the heavy traffic. Sean quickly walked into the bar nearby and moved through to exit out a back alley. This afforded him access to some of the back streets to Janey's 'bungalow.'

When Sean reached her residence, he stayed in the shadows. Her house was one of five residences facing a dead-end court. There was parking on the street and each residence had a short drive for one vehicle. These small brick homes had been built in the 1920s and were set amongst heavy foliage and trees. Sean was able to put himself on the ground next to an oak tree shielding him from the street but allowing a view of Janey's house.

Now Sean started removing his suit jacket. The pain was intense, but he knew that if an artery had been hit, he would be dead. His white shirt was soaked in blood, but his wound did not seem to be bleeding profusely. Leaving the jacket on with the shirt underneath had helped staunch the bleeding.

As Sean was trying to explore the extent of his wound, he saw the headlights of a car coming into the court. He stayed against the tree, pulled his knees up to his chest, and tried to keep his profile low.

With great relief, Sean recognized Janey's blue Mustang. He checked to see if any cars were coming down the street or any men were going to the house. Janey left the car and went into the house. Sean cautiously approached the heavy wooden door with a little window at the top. He gently knocked and Janey's face appeared at the window. She looked relieved to see him and opened the door.

A look of shock came over Janey's face when she saw Sean in the light. He immediately closed the front door.

"What the hell happened to you?"

As Sean worked his way to her bathroom, he mumbled, "I have been shot."

In the bathroom, Sean sat on the toilet and Janey grabbed some scissors.

As she cut away the shirt, she said "Let's see what we are dealing with here." As she washed off the blood with a washcloth, she examined the shoulder wound.

"Looks like the bullet passed through. There is an entrance and exit wound, and no bones or arteries were hit.

"Appears to be a large caliber bullet, probably a nine-millimeter. The exit wound is larger and needs to be stitched. Let's get you to an emergency room."

Sean was taken aback by her straight forward expertise. "I can't go to any hospital emergency room or any doc in a box. Whoever shot me will be looking for that. Besides, I do not want to answer questions."

While Janey used alcohol to clean the wounds, Sean gave her a rundown of what had happened, while clenching his teeth from the pain. He did not tell her everything but enough for her to understand the danger of the situation.

Janey silently looked at the torn flesh in Sean's shoulder, then left the room. When she reappeared, she had some needles and light-colored thread. She pulled a lighter and ran the flame over the needles.

"I am going to sew your holes closed. As you are aware, I do quite a bit of sewing, and even if I say so myself, I am a pretty good seamstress. First, you need to hit the scotch bottle for a little anesthesia."

Sean looked at the bottle of Dewars and said, "Not my usual

pour, but it will do." He took a big swig and put on his bravest face. "Let's do this."

Janey cleaned the wounds with hydrogen peroxide and the wounds bubbled. As she began meticulously stitching the back hole, Sean conversed between swigs of scotch.

"Where did you learn to take care of wounds like this?"

"I told you that I had a nursing degree from Louisiana Tech. Well, I was an operative nurse at an emergency room in Baton Rouge for a couple of years. I intended to get my registered nurse accreditation but the blood and guts got to me. So I decided to take a break and make some money in Houston."

Sean smiled. "I am glad you did."

When Janey finished the back wound, she moved to the front and closed it with a couple of stitches. She then put large sterile pads with white hospital tape. Sean felt like he could not have been better treated at any clinic in Houston.

Janey was looking through her medicine cabinet and came out with some pills. "Here is some Erythromycin I had left from a sinus infection. Take two now and we will use the rest as need be."

Sean felt exhausted from the stress, the pain, and the scotch, but he knew they could not be complacent.

"I have to get out of here. You are in danger with me here. Going to the police is out of the question. I have to get somewhere away from here to figure things out."

Janey calmly said, "I will take you. If we leave before they come here, we will get a head start and you can go anywhere."

Sean gravely said, "I appreciate your offer, but I can't let you risk this. I will get a rental car."

Janey got angry. "This is not negotiable. You know that what I am offering is the only real solution. In fact, I know where we can go. Remember I told you that I have family in the bayous of Louisiana. My uncle has a cabin that he would let his favorite niece use anytime. Believe me, no one will find us down there." Sean realized that she was right. He was lucky to have the help.

"Okay. Get some clothes together for a least a week. Then, I need to go by my house and get some clothes and money. I suggest we take a nap and get going about three in the morning.

"Meanwhile, can you make me a sandwich? I am starved. Let's see if the news has any stories on what happened at my office.

"You also need to make any calls to your family now and write down any numbers you will need. Your phone is going to have to remain in the house."

Janey shrugged her shoulders and went to make some sandwiches.

Chapter Thirteen
On the Run

Three o'clock in the morning came awfully early. When Sean awoke, his shoulder was throbbing and he felt woozy. He thought some Advil and coffee would make things right.

Janey had packed a bag and was watering plants and getting the house ready for an extended vacation.

"How long do you think we will be gone, Sean?"

"I don't have a clue. Once we are out of the crosshairs, I will try to do some digging for answers."

Not long after this exchange, the two of them were out the door. Janey seemed concerned about something.

"Can I leave a note for my neighbor and tell her to watch the place?"

"Afraid not. We will call after we are free from here, so bring her number."

Driving through the Montrose area at 3 A.M., there were a considerable number of people hanging out and partying. As Janey drove, Sean kept an eye out for the black Escalade. He knew they were out there. Janey drove through town toward the westside where Sean's house was located. When they approached his neighborhood, she parked one street over. Sean told her to wait half an hour and if he was not back to drive by his house then go to the cops if she didn't see him.

This area of Houston used to consist of one-story ranch-style homes. Now the majority of the lots had huge houses on the large lots. Due to the similarity in style and size, Sean thought of them as "McMansions."

Sean's home was an updated ranch and he was happy with it that way. All of the homes were set thirty feet from the street and there was an abundance of big trees. This allowed him to move in shadows from house to house and avoid the street. When he was two lots away, he stopped to see if there was any movement or if anything did not look right. When he satisfied himself that it appeared safe, he crossed his lot and went to the garden gate to go to the rear of the house. As he was inserting his key, he noticed that the door had been jacked open.

Sean immediately moved to the corner of his back porch away from the light. Sean thought about the situation. *Would the hit men stay at the house or vacate when it was apparent he was not home?* The latter seemed the most likely, but he could enter through his garage. Then again, that might be the entrance they'd expect him to come in. Better to go in the same way as them. Sean did pick up a rebar rod he used for gardening, so he did not feel defenseless.

Sean pushed the door open with his left hand and held the rod in his right hand. He slowly worked his way into the kitchen. He placed the rod on the counter and grabbed a big butcher knife. The house was dead quiet, except for the central air conditioning system blowing through the vents. Sean moved down the hall to his bedroom and grabbed his police style .38, loaded with hollow-point bullets. At least now, I have a chance, thought Sean. As he moved room to room, there was no sign of his house having been entered.

Sean grabbed a duffle bag and put underwear, socks, jeans, shorts, shirts, and a pair of comfortable shoes. He quickly changed into blue jeans and dark blue Polo shirt. It was a relief to get out of the suit pants and the ragged t-shirt he borrowed from Janey. He put everything in a bag and put it in the garage.

His final mission was to retrieve some cash. Sean had put away the majority of the $30,000 the cartel gave him in Laredo. He pulled down the attic stairs and pushed up some insulation that was laid down up there. He retrieved a brown manila envelope and put it in his duffle bag. *That should cover us for a while,* thought Sean.

After putting the stairs back, Sean checked around the house and got ready to leave. He put the pistol under his belt in the small of his back and wore the shirt out to conceal the gun.

Sean exited through the same door so that it would look like he had not been here, or so he hoped. There was no doubt in his mind that these hitmen (as he liked to think of them) would be back looking for him.

Sean went back down the street exactly as he had come and arrived at Janey's car just under the half hour he planned.

"I am so glad to see you. I did not know what I would have done if you had not come back."

Sean pulled the gun out of his back waistband. "You need to do what I said. Go to the cops."

Janey looked perplexed. "Why aren't we going now?"

"I cannot trust any cops or government people. Besides, after I tell them what happened, we are on our own again. There won't be protection from the cops. We need to protect ourselves.

"Time to go to Louisiana. Let's stop at a Wal-Mart outside Beaumont and buy a couple of burner phones. I brought about $25,000 from the house so we have cash for a while. Remember, do not use any credit cards."

Janey shook her head knowingly. She then moved the Mustang toward Interstate 10 East to get out of town. Sean believed the multiple highways of Houston would confuse any plan to intercept him, since they went in every direction of the compass.

They made it to Beaumont at about 6 A.M. and found a Wal-Mart right off the freeway. Janey went in and purchased four burner phones, with cash, so that they could make the necessary calls and then ditch the phones.

After securing some breakfast sandwiches and coffee, Sean directed Janey to a roadside park just outside of Beaumont. Even though it was early, it was time to call some people. First on the list was Janey's uncle to see if his cabin was available. Janey knew that he went fishing early and he was awake. He was glad to hear from her and told her to stay there. The key was in its usual hiding place—the mouth of a fish on the front porch. He refreshed her recollection on the directions (even Google maps, if they had it on the burner phones, would not find the place). Her uncle said he would be by there in the next day or so to check on things.

Next on the priority list was calling his secretary Maria. Sean realized she was just awaking, but this was an emergency.

He explained that he would not be around for a while and she needed to continue any cases he had on the docket for the next couple weeks. Sean also explained that he no longer had his phone and was using a burner phone. He would call her but she could not reach him. Maria told him that the shooting was all over the local news and two bodies were found at the building, but no identification was made. Sean deduced that John Valenti had made it out and probably lost one, or two, bodyguards. Most likely, Valenti took out one of the assassins as well.

Sean told Maria that he wanted the direct number for Joe Paggione, the federal prosecutor. She promised to be at the office in an hour, and Sean said he would call again then. At the last minute, he also asked for the number of Mr. Green, the assistant of Lou Cicero. She promised to look for it as well.

Sean ate his egg sandwiches like a ravenous dog. Being on the run was working up a big appetite. After the meal, Sean indicated it was time to go. He was constantly looking for black SUVs and felt uneasy being so close to the freeway. Maybe he was paranoid, but that was what getting shot at would do to you.

As they resumed traveling on East Interstate 10, Janey asked, "Why are you contacting Cicero's people? Aren't they the same thugs who may be trying to kill you?"

"I need some answers and Lou Cicero is as connected as anyone. Yes, he is a mafia boss, but he has a separate family from Valenti. I believe that he would not want to see anything happen to me. I have been his lawyer for a long time and he trusts me. Besides, I have to trust someone."

"What about the federal prosecutor? I thought you were avoiding anything with the cops or the government?"

"Again, I have to place trust in select places to get some answers. Joe has proven to me that he is honest and trustworthy. He is also very smart and street savvy, so he can dig out what is the truth. I believe he will also understand my reticence in not going to the authorities. Besides, I am calling from a burner phone that won't be around long enough to get a fix on our locale."

When they reached Lake Charles, Sean instructed Janey to drive to the Golden Nugget Casino. This area was very popular with Texans and had two big casinos. Sean figured they would park in the huge parking lot to hide from detection while he made his other calls. True to form, the massive parking lot was filled with vehicles with Texas license plates. They found a space between a F-150 truck and a Lexus SUV which sheltered the smaller Mustang.

Sean again called Maria on her cell phone. He could not chance the office phone. Maria was distraught when he talked to her. She explained that the homicide detectives were in the office when she arrived. When she asked the lieutenant why they were in the office, he explained that the building management let him in to investigate the shooting. Maria said that no shooting occurred in the office, and they did not have a warrant, so he needed to leave. She said the lieutenant was upset and told her he would return with a warrant.

Sean praised her for handling the situation so well. She found the numbers for Joe Paggione and Mr. Green, and Sean wrote the numbers on a legal pad Janey brought with them. Sean's parting words to Maria were to say as little as possible, but not to lie to the cops. Sean was not going to tell her his location, so she could not give that information to the authorities. He told her that he would call her in the next couple of days.

Sean's next call was to Joe Paggione. It was almost 9 A.M. and he knew that the federal prosecutors usually went to their office before the 10 A.M. federal docket. He guessed right because Paggione picked up the call.

"Paggione here."

"Joe, this is Sean Braxton. There has been an incident at my building last night and I need some help."

"No shit. Two people are dead, and you are missing."

"There is a reason for that. Someone tried to shoot me with an automatic weapon from a black Escalade."

"My information says that these guys were after Valenti but missed him."

"Joe, they were trying to shoot me as well. Who are the dead guys?"

"It appears one is a cartel hit man from Mexico. The other is an old associate of the Valenti family."

That is what Sean figured. "Can you tell me anything about Valenti?"

"He is gone with the wind. Needless to say, I think the cops and the FBI would like to talk with you and your client."

Sean hesitated, then said, "Not going to happen for a while. I cannot trust putting myself into the hands of the government. Before you give me your platitudes, remember what happened to your witness in federal protection. Further, I know that the Valentis have access to government information. Probably someone on their payroll."

Joe sighed. "I suppose you are justified in not trusting anyone now, but I will work on protection for you. We need to talk face to face."

"That is not going to happen for a while. It is Wednesday so I will call you again on Friday morning, same time. See if you can't get your agents to fill in the blanks. Talk to you then."

Sean knew that there was a risk calling back at a set time, but it was a risk worth taking to get some answers.

Sean next called Mr. Green. The call went to voice mail, which was not unusual. "This is Sean Braxton. Please take a message to our friend. I am out of town with no way to be reached. I need information and protection. Deliver any information to my secretary Maria. I will be in contact with her."

After he finished the last call, he realized that Janey was just staring at him.

"You mean that you are pushing the authorities to the side while you embrace the mafia. What the fuck?"

"As I told you, the true answers will come from Cicero and his people. He will know who is behind this and how to deal with it. So long as we are safe, I can weigh the options. So, let's get to the safe spot."

Janey started leaving the lot when Sean directed her to a nearby garbage can. He exited the car and dumped the phone he had been using in the garbage can.

Interstate 10 cut through southern Louisiana and crossed numerous waterways, many with huge cedars and oaks. Spanish moss hung from the trees, giving the effect of a primordial forest.

Shortly after a road sign indicating Baton Rouge in forty-five miles, Janey exited on a two-lane highway. They traveled on the highway for almost twenty miles and turned at a sign indicating Bayou Grosse Tete.

Janey said, "We are in Iberville Parish and the cabin is on the Grosse Tete away from any towns. The cabin turnoff is just ahead."

Janey turned down a dirt track that had sand and stones that indicated it was a useable road. After they turned in, the woods seemed to swallow the Mustang. After a half mile, they arrived at a very rustic wood cabin. It looked well maintained, but the cedar shell of the cabin was bleached and aged. Janey parked the Mustang next to the cabin and got out. She went on the porch and retrieved the key from the mouth of a big largemouth bass mounted next to the door.

They entered the cabin. It had rustic furniture—an overstuffed couch, a wooden table with four chairs, and a big leather chair with a reading light. There were shelves loaded with books on one wall.

Janey said, "Our first order of business is to start the generator out back. That will supply our power and water."

Sean went back behind the cabin with Janey and entered an old shed. She found a flashlight inside the door and turned it on. They found a big can of diesel fuel and a funnel to help pour the fuel into the generator tanks.

Sean was expecting a pull start for the generator but found it had an electric start. After Janey pushed the button, the generator hummed to life. Sean noted that it was not as bad as he expected.

When they reentered the cabin, a couple lights started flickering. He inspected the bedroom which had a nice double bed in a hand-hewn wood frame. Sean thought that this might be a good escape. Too bad they had crazies on their tail.

Janey told Sean to get acquainted with the area and she left to go buy groceries in town. Sean gave her $1,000 and told her to spend whatever she needed.

Sean started walking around the woods surrounding the cabin. The trees were old and huge, mainly oaks. The underbrush was not too thick because the forest canopy was so thick. It was dark with only filtered sun. It was so quiet that the only sound was his footsteps in the leaves. He eventually came upon the bayou, which was basically a slow moving stream. The water was brown from the tannins, but remarkably clear. Cattails and lily pads made the placid water look especially inviting for bass fishing. Sean had a weakness for fishing and would do it whenever possible. He was not sure how his shoulder would react to fishing, but he was game to find out.

Sean continued his walk around the property and saw deer, wild boars, and nutria, a giant water-loving rat. It was a relaxing place to get his mind straight. Now that he could clear his brain, he went over the shooting again. There was no doubt in his mind that the 'hit-men' were after him, as well as Valenti. As for a reason, all he could think was that John Valenti's Uncle Augie had Sean equated with John. It stood to reason that the uncle might have believed that Sean was acting as the consigliere to John's break-away family. This would put a price on his head and a target on his back. He had to get Lou Cicero to straighten out this misinformation if he would be willing to do so.

Sean worked his way back to the cabin without realizing it. Janey's Mustang was parked out front. When Sean entered the cabin, Janey was putting groceries away in the cabinet and the refrigerator. Along with food, she had picked up some beer, wine, and a fifth of Johnnie Walker Black. Sean reached for the bottle and poured a glass.

"Care to join me?"

Janey replied, "I will have something softer in a minute. There are steaks for tonight, if you will grill. I bought charcoal and there is a grill behind the cabin."

"That sounds wonderful. You seem to have all the amenities of the big city."

"I went to the bigger town of Plaquemine to get the booze and shop at the bigger food store. The town of Indian Village is closer but does not have much there."

Sean went out and sat on the porch in one of the two rocking chairs, enjoying his drink and the solitude. Janey came out to join him with a beer.

Sean turned to Janey and said, "This was the perfect idea for a get-away. I feel relaxed and don't have that feeling of impending doom."

Janey smiled, "Glad I could oblige. This cabin has always been a refuge for me. Uncle Bubbie never had any kids and I was the favorite niece. I was always a bit of a tomboy, and he took me fishing and hunting. Since I grew up in Baton Rouge, this was an easy escape."

After grilling the steaks, and splitting a bottle of cabernet, Sean felt the need to crash. He helped Janey clean up then they retired to the bed. They had slow, easy sex. Sean was conscious of the pain in his shoulder but the liquor had subdued the pain enough for him to enjoy Janey's exquisite body and technique.

After they climaxed and cleaned up, they immediately went to sleep.

The next morning started slowly with Sean enjoying his coffee on the front porch and Janey sleeping late. There were numerous song birds around and their voices sweetened the air. Sean realized it has been a while since he really enjoyed being in nature. At least getting shot at had one redeeming quality. He also realized how lucky he was to have Janey and her access to this slice of paradise.

While Sean was enjoying his perch on the pond, a big Ram pickup truck drove up and parked next to the Janey's Mustang. Sean had the pistol on the table next to him and he slowly put his hand on top of the gun. A big bear of a man got out of the truck. He was not tall, but stocky and muscular with a bushy handlebar mustache.

Sean knew by the mustache that this was Uncle Bubbie. That was the one feature Janey described. He approached Sean with a smile and his hand extended.

"Ya must be Janey's friend. She said that y'all were coming by."

"My name is Sean and you are her Uncle Bubbie, right?

"Call me Bubba. Bubbie was a family nickname."

Bubba stepped on the porch and sat down. Sean offered coffee and Bubba accepted. As Sean was putting the cups on the little table, Bubba started talking.

"My guess is that Janey is still asleep. That girl will stay out for twelve hours if you let her. Always been like that."

Just then Janey came out the screen door. "I need my beauty sleep, don't I?"

"Darlin, you are too pretty as it is. How are ya?"

The uncle and niece embraced and kissed each other on the cheeks. Janey went in and got a cup of coffee, and Sean grabbed a chair from the table inside.

Once everyone was situated, Bubba began the conversation.

"I don't believe y'all are here to enjoy the woods. Tell me what is going on."

Sean explained he was a criminal defense attorney and that one of his clients got crosswise with a mob boss. He related the circumstance with getting ambushed outside his office leaving with the client. He also emphasized that he knew he was a target as well as his client.

Bubba intervened, "I know that it involves the Valenti family from Kansas City. Even us backwoods Cajuns watch the news. I imagine you do not have your cell phones with you. It's like having a beacon."

"No. Both Janey and I left our cell phones, and we picked up some burner phones. Started with four and have three left."

"Smart. You think they will continue after you even with the possibility of the dead Valenti nephew and the machine gun play outside your building?"

"I am certain of it. We are dealing with the Mafia and my guess is cartel hitmen. They don't quit and don't give a shit about the press accounts."

Bubba sat back in the chair and downed his coffee cup. "I have done my share of smuggling. Our family made moonshine, smuggled booze during prohibition, and continued with pot and coke. I have had my times with those cartel guys and you are right. They are ruthless and dangerous. You were right to get off the grid down here. We know how to protect our own in these bayous."

Sean was surprised to hear Bubba talk about his smuggling but Janey had told him that the La Plante family was known throughout the bayous as the ones to come to for whatever you need. Janey said both her father and her uncle had been involved in the family business. Janey's father and mother were killed on a Louisiana highway ten years ago and Uncle Bubbie was the closest family she had left.

Bubba now asked, "I assume you are going to be making some more calls. You won't get any service here and if someone pinpoints your locale, it should not be here. My suggestion is you run into Indian Village and call there. I have the rest of the day free if y'all would like to do some fishing."

Janey said, "Thanks, but I am just going to relax, but I know Sean loves fishing."

Sean jumped at the opportunity to go fishing. Bubba went to a little shed behind the cabin and retrieved a couple rods. Bubba explained that he had a boat in a boathouse on the far reach of the property on the bayou. As Bubba and Sean were preparing to leave, Bubba said to Janey, "Your cousin John wants to have a fais do-do tonight to welcome you back. What say?"

Sean interrupted and asked, "What is a fais do-do?"

Bubba laughed, "That is what us coon-asses call a party. Sometimes music and dancing, but always lots of food and booze."

Sean looked at Janey and shrugged. She said, "We are in. Do I need to bring any food?"

"No. The locals will bring the crawdads, shrimp, and whatever else. Just bring your appetites."

Bubba and Sean spent most of the day fishing the bayou and

the river. They caught largemouth bass and big catfish. Bubba said that it would all go in the pot for the party. He even shot a possum for the "pot."

After fishing, Bubba and Sean came back to pick up Janey. Sean wanted to shower, but Bubba just looked at him, and motioned to leave.

Bubba drove blue highways that seemed to snake around the many bayous and ponds. There were few road signs, but Bubba drove so fast you couldn't see the signs anyway. They finally came to a nice ranch style house sitting on a pretty stretch of water.

Janey jumped from the truck and ran up to the tall, lanky man crossing the yard. They hugged and kissed cheeks, which Sean noted to be the standard family greeting. A woman with dark skin and dark hair came out of the house and was introduced as John's wife, Mabel. Janey greeted her with kisses as well. When Sean approached Mabel with an outstretched hand, she bypassed it, hugged him, and kissed his cheeks.

John and Mabel took Sean and Janey to a party shed behind their house. It was built with aged cedar, had a bar with neon beer signs, multiple picnic tables and enough room for many people. While Bubba was off cleaning the fish, John and Mabel asked why Sean and Janey were down in the bayous. Janey took the lead and said, "I thought that my boyfriend should see where his Cajun girlfriend's family resides."

John said, "When he meets all these coon-ass relatives, he might never come back."

Sean smiled and said, "So far I can't see a reason to go back to Houston."

Gradually more and more people showed up. Some were family but most friends on the bayou. Everyone seemed to bring something: venison, wild boar chops, squirrel, crawfish, shrimp, and even a bucket of frog legs. Some of the bigger cuts of meat were seasoned and put on a charcoal grill. Much of the rest was thrown into a simmering cast iron pot, big enough to hold anything they put in. The smell of the peppers and spices was enough to make Sean's eyes water.

Sean found a seat at one of the tables and sipped a Dixie beer. Many people came by and talked to him. Some had accents so heavy he had a hard time understanding. The one constant factor was how nice everyone was to him, even when Bubba told them he was "one of them goddamn trial lawyers."

The party continued for hours, and Sean enjoyed the spicy food and the cold Dixie beer. Around midnight, Bubba came to Sean and Janey to round them up. Sean thanked John and Mabel and told them truthfully that it was one of the best parties he had been to.

Sean was astounded that Bubba could drive back through the pitch-black forest with such skill. When they arrived at the cabin, he pulled Sean aside.

"I don't want you getting my niece in the cross hairs of these scumbags. Let her mind the cabin when you leave. I am going to go see whether any dark visitors have been in our parish. I will be back to check on y'all."

Bubba then drove away. Sean and Janey retreated to the bedroom, intoxicated and happy.

Chapter Fourteen
Sanctuary

The next morning, Sean and Janey started slow but then Sean remembered he had to call Joe Paggione at the United States Attorney's office before ten. Sean's shoulder was throbbing from the activity the day before. Janey examined the wound and thought it was healing well. She cleaned it again with alcohol and put on a fresh bandage so they could go to Indian Village. Sean grabbed another one of the burner phones and they jumped in the Mustang.

The route to Indian Village was different than any way they had previously traveled. Along with the woods and bayous, they traveled by some aqua farms raising crawdads amid rice-fields. *These Cajuns do love those mudbugs,* thought Sean. They passed a few traditional farms as well with cattle, pigs, and sheep. Although the dwellings were not impressive, the usual one-story house or trailer looked well cared for.

Indian Village was not even a real town, per se. It was a collection of dwellings and historical structures, some dating back to the late 1600s. There was good cell phone reception here though and it was remote. They found a general store and parked in the dirt parking lot. Sean called Joe Paggione since it was almost 9:45. He answered immediately.

"I was getting concerned about hearing from you. It appears you are a popular guy right now. Houston Police want to talk with you regarding the two stiffs and it appears you were targeted. There was also blood found on the second floor of the parking garage not related to either of the dead guys. Is that you?"

Sean carefully replied, "Yes, I got a minor cut trying to dodge the bullets. No big deal." Sean did not want to let on that he had been shot.

"I am not sure I believe you. There was a trail of blood going down and out of the garage. Don't be a fool about this."

"I know what I am doing Joe. Tell me what leads you to say I was a target."

"The Kansas City FBI picked up some statements by Valenti Family members that the 'old man' was taking out John and his lawyer. They also heard that the job was handed to some Mexican cartel group. Does that accord with what you saw?"

"My brief view of the shooters was dark-skinned Mexicans with Mac-10 automatics."

"That would fit the bill for cartel hit men all right. Not much else to report. You are going to have to come in at some point. Why not now? These dogs will keep on the hunt."

"Not just yet. I feel safe now and will let you know something soon. Thanks for the help." Sean clicked off the phone and looked at Janey.

"It is Uncle Augie and he has targeted me along with John. He is also using Mexican cartel hit men. This just confirms what I thought anyway."

146

Janey looked ready to cry and Sean hugged her.

"Don't worry. We are safe now and I will figure something out." He kissed her forehead and she gave a half smile.

Next on the phone agenda was to call Mr. Green for access to Lou Cicero. Mr. Green answered by the second ring. As usual, he was brief and to the point.

"Our friend wanted you to know that he is aware of the problems, and he is working to resolve matters. Be prepared to meet with those concerned. Time and place will be relayed to you within the next couple of days."

Sean quickly cut in before he could hang up. "You do realize that this is a non-working number after today."

"This is Friday. Contact your office on Monday and there should be a message from our friend."

With that last statement, Mr. Green hung up. Sean was hoping for more, but knowing how Cicero operates he was not surprised. Janey, however, was a little vexed.

"You mean that is all the information you get. A one-minute call with no help, and no protection. It looks like Cicero is cutting you loose."

Sean tried to calm her down. "This is how Cicero does his business. All information is third hand, particularly over a telephone. I know him and he will step up. We just have to give him a little time."

Sean's last call was to Maria at the office. She gave him a brief summary on the status of his cases, and Sean told her to contact one of his other defense counsel friends to fill in for him on any pressing matters. She also said that the homicide cops were coming by every day and threatening to put her in jail if she didn't give them his location. Sean told her to have one of the lawyers in the office deal with them. He assured her that they could not arrest her for something she did not know.

Finally, Sean told her. "I believe on Monday you will be provided some information by Mr. Green. That is important and might be the key to getting me out of this mess. I take it you have not heard from Valenti either. Didn't think so. Okay. Be tough. I will be in touch in the next day or so."

Sean hung up and looked at Janey.

"Would you like to call anyone?"

She requested to call her neighbor. He told her to keep it very brief. Janey took the phone and wandered away. In a couple minutes she returned.

"My neighbor said that there was a Cadillac Escalade that has come in to the cul-de-sac a couple times. I told her to call the cops if they see it again."

Sean nodded his head in assent. "That is the right move. Those thugs do not want to fade any heat."

"If there are no other calls to make, time to deep six this phone." Sean walked over to the bridge they crossed to get into Indian Village and threw the phone into the bayou. Sean returned to the Mustang and they then drove back to the safety of the cabin.

Sean and Janey spent the remainder of the day reading and relaxing. Their abode felt so remote and hidden that their worries were suppressed. It was a good feeling.

Late in the afternoon, Bubba came to visit. He asked if they had made the phone calls and where they were when they made the calls. Bubba was glad they had used Indian Village. After getting this information, Bubba left again and told them he would be back in touch. This being Friday night, Sean proposed that they grill the steaks she had picked up and make it a date night. His idea was to create some normalcy to ease the pressure.

Along with the steaks, they cooked some asparagus and tossed a salad. Janey had purchased a nice Merlot that they shared with the meal.

During the dinner, Janey asked Sean, "Does this mess change your mind on practicing criminal defense in the future?"

Sean tried to be glib. "If I am dead, I guess that would end my career. Being serious though, this escapade has made me question my career path. I had always thought that the danger in representing organized crime figures was the government coming after me as the lawyer. Even if I stay out of their business, representing the crime boss can have tangential pitfalls.

"To answer your question, I may need to reexamine my field of practice, but I need some distance and perspective. I am too close and affected by the immediate danger to analyze clearly."

Janey smiled and said, "That was a convoluted way to say maybe."

"Lawyers are good at not answering questions and providing circular responses. I am what I have been trained to be."

After cleaning up the dinner, Sean and Janey shared the rest of the wine then returned to make slow, easy love. Even with his shoulder pain, Sean enjoyed Janey more than ever. He realized that she was the best woman of his life.

The next morning Sean got up and took a walkabout on the property. He was really beginning to feel more relaxed. Being out in nature had calmed him in the past and helped provide clarity of thought.

Sean believed his analysis of the problem with Augie Valenti and the solution was sound. He knew that Lou Cicero could calm the waters and get Augie to pull back. He would also be able to reach John Valenti. Hopefully, Cicero might be able to broker a deal.

Sean had been walking for a while, when he realized he had circled back to the cabin. He noticed Bubba's big truck was there.

Bubba was sitting on the porch talking with Janey. Sean walked up and volunteered to cook some breakfast. He had been a 'short order' breakfast cook when he went to college and enjoyed the simple pleasure of frying bacon, cooking eggs in the grease, and burning some toast. He finished and set the table.

While they were eating, Bubba remarked on what he had been doing since they saw him yesterday.

"I have been touching base with my coon-ass underground network. This here is a small parish and the swamp people know when an outsider is around the parish.

"I got a gut feeling that those Mexicans are coming here. Not to the cabin, but around the parish. There is no word yet, but I got my sawed-off twelve gauge next to my seat and hope I see those fucks."

Janey said, "Uncle Bubbie, do you think we are safe here?"

"There is no place safer. No one will know how to find this cabin. It is when these guys come searching that they go from being the spider to the fly. I need them to get caught in the web.

"That brings up a point. Do not go anywhere today or to-morrow. I do not want any chance for you to run into those clowns. Just enjoy the day and the woods around the cabin."

Bubba stood up and prepared to leave. Janey started clearing the dishes and Bubba motioned to Sean to go outside with him.

He turned to Sean and said in a low voice. "Keep the pistol with you at all times. I don't think there is much of a chance these boys could find this cabin, but you never know."

Bubba got up into the truck. He told Sean that he would come back later tomorrow. Bubba drove the truck back out toward the highway.

Bubba figured that these dogs would still be driving the black Cadillac Escalade. No reason to change their ride. If he did find their vehicle, he figured that there would probably be two or three of them together.

Bubba stopped by and visited with the Dupree brothers, who were the biggest dope distributors in the parish. He told them that he had word some Mexicans were trying to bring their dope into the Dupree Territory. That sent the brothers into a fever. They started touching base with their dealers. This put eyes and ears all through the parish. Bubba told them to let him know immediately if they found these Mexicans, because he had un-finished business with them.

Bubba also decided to hedge his bet, and notified his cousin Benjy, who was a Sheriff's Deputy in the parish. He told him about the vehicle and that there were armed cartel members around. He told him to keep his eyes open and his mouth shut.

No word came to Bubba from any of his contacts on Saturday. So early Sunday morning, he picked up some Voodoo donuts and went over to the cabin to check on Janey and Sean. He had to admit to himself that Janey had found a good man, although he was not usually fond of lawyers. Sean had enough of a twist to his character that he liked him and did not want to see him hurt. Besides, it might be good to have a criminal defense lawyer in the family.

When he arrived at the cabin, Sean was sitting on the porch drinking coffee. As Bubba approached, he told Sean that he had some Voodoo donuts.

"What the hell are Voodoo donuts? Are they cursed?"

"Nothing like that. They are just good donuts with an unusual name. How was your day yesterday?"

Sean chewed his bite of the donut, then said, "That is really good. We just enjoyed being around here. It is very relaxing. How about you? Any word on the cartel guys?"

"No. I have put out the word but nothing yet." At that moment, Bubba heard the ping of his phone indicating a text. He pulled his phone from his pocket and found a text from one of the Dupree brothers.

"There is a Black Escalade out near Indian Village. Hard to see inside with tinted windows. One of them went into the gas station store and was a dark-skinned Mexican."

Bubba texted back. "Hold tight. I am on my way over there."

Bubba looked at Sean.

"There is something I need to do. Y'all stay here until I tell you otherwise."

Bubba went out and got in the truck. Sean followed him out. "Is it the hit men? Should I come?"

"That would be the stupidest thing to do. Stay here."

With that, Bubba tore down the road envisioning how to work things. These guys were professional killers and would be well armed. Bubba had his sawed-off 12 gauge and a Glock 9-millimeter hand gun. Not enough offense against automatic weapons. Bubba decided he had to get his cousin, Benjy, involved.

"Benjy, those Mexican cartel guys are out near Indian Village. Are you on patrol? Good. Get your ass over there and be loaded for bear."

When Bubba made it near Indian Village, he slowed down to peruse the side roads and driveways. Indian Village had one way in and out across the bridge over the bayou. Bubba slowly crossed the bridge looking around the center of town. As he drove down the main, and only, street he spotted the Escalade parked in the dirt lot next to the store. Bubba kept on driving to the far end of town but noticed the Texas license plates as he drove by.

Bubba parked in the driveway of an abandoned house overgrown with vines. He had a view down into town. He called his cousin again.

"They are parked by the store in Indian Village. I am going to drive back out and across the bridge. You go in to town, and if my guess is right, your cop car will make them move. When they try to cross the bridge, I will block it."

Benjy said, "I am about five minutes away."

"I will go back across the bridge now and look for you. Be

careful. These guys have automatics and are not afraid to use them."

"10-4. Watch your ass too, Bubba."

Bubba had been in his share of scrapes and had been shot at before, but he knew this would be different.

Bubba again passed the Escalade and looked right at it but could not see inside. He kept driving and crossed the bridge, going about hundred yards down to a nearby driveway, and parked.

Bubba called Benjy. "You need to slowly drive by the Escalade and continue down into town, then turn around. I am betting they will move once you are parked. I will block them on the far side of the bridge."

Shortly after Bubba hung up, he saw Benjy in his Sheriff Department vehicle go by. Bubba quietly said to himself, "It's rodeo time." He watched Benjy cross the bridge and then he slowly drove out. True to what he expected, after Benjy's patrol car passed by the Escalade, they pulled out of the store parking lot and headed for the bridge.

Bubba approached from the opposite way, and when they were both on the bridge, he turned his truck to block both lanes. The passenger side was facing the Escalade.

The windows went down on the passenger side of the Escalade and a dark figure emerged holding a small automatic. Bubba had been waiting for an action like this and he fired his two-shot sawed off shotgun at the guy out the window and at the driver's side of the windshield. Bubba did not know whether he hit either the driver or the passenger, but the unexpected blasts caused the driver to serve right into the wooden guardrail on the old bridge. The guardrails collapsed from the impact. The Escalade tumbled off the bridge in slow motion and splashed into the chocolate brown water of the bayou.

Benjy was at the other end of the bridge and out of his vehicle with a standard shotgun. Bubba dropped the shotgun he was carrying and pulled his Glock handgun. They both went to the railing on the side of the bridge and looked down. The passenger had escaped out his open window and shot a burst from his Mac-10 in Bubba's direction. The guy was floundering in the water and his shots were misdirected. Benjy shot the twelve-gauge at the passenger and he went under water, then, bobbed up face down, carried away by the current.

There was no sign from the other occupants. Bubba scrambled down the bank to the vehicle slowly sinking in the water. He yelled to Benjy, "Cover me. I am going to try and get those guys out."

Bubba could barely make out the driver with his head resting on the steering wheel. No sign of anyone else though. Bubba went into the water and side stroked to the driver side door, holding the gun in front. When he reached the driver's side window, he tried breaking the glass with the butt of the gun with no success. Bubba then shot the upper corner of the window away from the driver and the glass shattered. The Escalade was going down faster now. Bubba reached in and grabbed the driver by his shirt collar. He was not seat belted in. Bubba was able to pull him out and get him to the shore.

Benjy was waiting on the shore and helped them out. The driver started coming around, Bubba flipped him on his stomach and Benjy handcuffed his hands behind his back. Benjy looked at Bubba and smiled.

"That was awful brave. Are there any others?"

"I did not see anyone behind the seat. Besides, it may be too late anyway."

They both looked on as the Escalade settled down under the waterline. The bayou was only ten to twelve feet deep here, but that was sufficient.

Benjy said, "I called for backup and we should see activity soon."

Bubba looked at the driver who was starting to realize what was going on. Bubba asked, "Cuanto personas en el Escalade?"

The driver answered, "Dos."

Bubba looked at Benjy. "He says two, so that would account for both."

Benjy picked up his radio and called to one of the support cars coming to check downstream for the other guy. Benjy grabbed the handcuffed driver by the arm and took him up the slope to the patrol car. He put the handcuffed cartel hitman in the backseat, and to Bubba's eyes he now looked like a scared Mexican teenager.

As Bubba was drying off and changing into other clothes he kept in the truck, two other Sheriff vehicles appeared. He let them talk to Benjy for a while and then he walked over.

Benjy came over to Bubba.

"The Sheriff called for the dive team from the office and a heavy-duty wrecker to haul the car out of the bayou. I am going to say I shot the windshield and the shooter with the Mac-10.

"I have been told to get the driver checked out by EMS and

then put his ass in jail. This was a little hairy, but you handled it well."

Bubba smiled at the praise. "Keep my role as small as possible. You take the credit and glory."

While Benjy and Bubba were talking, one of the other deputies came up. "They found a body a couple hundred yards down the bayou. He showed signs of having been shot by a shotgun."

Benjy said, "He pulled an automatic on me. I had no choice. Did they find his weapon?"

"Not that I know of. The divers are coming and they can look. Besides, you have a witness." The deputy nodded his head at Bubba.

"That is right. If Benjy had not shot him, he would have killed both of us."

Bubba took Benjy aside, "I have to go back to see Janey and the guy she is with who these assholes were after. They need to be aware that someone knows they are in Iberville Parish."

Bubba hurried back to the cabin and related what happened.

Sean told Bubba, "Your bravery and smarts saved our asses. What do you think about the fact that they went to the location where we last called?"

"These burner phones still can be traced while the call is ongoing. I felt like your call to the United States Attorney's Office was the opportunity they needed."

Sean shook his head. "I still trust the Assistant United States attorney I know, but there is a leak. Tomorrow morning, I will call him again and give him the information on the shooters. One is dead, correct, and one other is in custody. The Feds can come see for themselves. We will need to be out of here though."

"I agree. Let's get your calls done tomorrow morning, then figure another course of action. I am going to go with you when you call. I will be here by 7:30 tomorrow morning.

"In the meantime, let's drink some of that scotch you told me about. I believe I am entitled to some whiskey."

The next morning at eight, Bubba was back at the cabin. Both Bubba and Sean were a little hungover from staying up and finishing the bottle of Johnnie Walker Black. They sat on the porch drinking coffee. Bubba started the conversation.

"I am going to drive you into Plaquemine to make your calls. That is also where the parish jail is located. I may check on the prisoner while you make your calls. Do you plan to let the feds know about the shooters?"

"I think that is the best course. I will inform the federal prosecutor who I know well. He can get a federal detainer on him for the automatic weapons, and I will bet for immigration as well."

"I am also going to find out if my other connections can get me out of the Valenti family mess. There should be some word on that."

"Sounds like a plan, Sean. Let's leave Janey here in case there are any other unforeseen problems."

Sean nodded and said, "Agreed."

Sean went into the bedroom and kissed the sleeping Janey on the forehead. She rose up enough for him to tell her he was off with Bubba. She grunted and went back to sleep.

Sean went over and retrieved one of two remaining burner phones and his list of phone numbers. While he was at it, he grabbed a few hundred dollars from the stash in the canvas carryall bag.

The drive to Plaquemine was direct and quick. After all, Bubba reminded him, this is the "Metropolis of Iberville Parish."

As they entered the city, Sean saw several mansions which appeared to be Victorian or pre-Civil War. They were mixed with modern day ranch style homes. It was a clean, small town.

Bubba drove up to a 1950s modern one-story building. The sign indicated it was the Iberville Parish Court. Bubba dropped Sean off in front of the building and told him to make his calls from one of the two benches by the courthouse.

"I can't think of any place safer. I am going to meet my cousin Benjy at the Sheriff's Department. See you in a half hour. You have my cell phone number if you need me."

Sean took a seat in a bench facing the street and one of the historic-looking houses. It was only nine, but Sean figured he would try Joe Paggione first. He picked up after one ring.

"Paggione."

"Hey Joe, this is Sean. I have some interesting news for you. Yesterday, the two cartel thugs were in a shootout with some police in Louisiana. One of them is dead and the other is in custody with the Iberville Parish Sheriff's Department."

"I'll be damned. That is good news for all concerned. How did this come about?"

"Let's say that I had a guardian angel who helped trap these guys for the cops and they got violent. No surprise, there?"

"Not at all. I will get someone from the FBI to go the parish jail today. So, I will take a wild guess that you are staying somewhere in the swamps and these boys came looking for you."

"Good guess, but they went to a town where I made my phone calls with a burner phone. My best guess is that they traced the call to a cell tower in Iberville Parish. I have to also say that it was likely out of your office."

"Wait a minute, Sean. Are you accusing me of providing information to these thugs?"

"No, not at all, Joe. But someone knew you took my call and even if they can't get my phone per se, they can trace it to a cellular area."

"Seems farfetched but plausible. I did tell the FBI case agents about our conversations. Possible... anyway, you are coming in now, right?"

"Not quite yet. I still have a problem that needs to be resolved first."

"I get it. We can offer you sanctuary."

"Forgive me if I beg off having the government protect me. Hope to talk soon."

With that, Sean hung up. He hoped that his theory of how the guys got his location stirred the hornet's nest at the Feds. Sean had a gut feeling that someone in the FBI was involved.

Sean called Maria at his office next. She picked up and said, "Call my cell."

Sean found the number on his sheet and called.

"What's up? Why the switch?"

"Mr. Green had a messenger bring a letter to me this morning. It specifically told me to convey this information by cell phone. This is what I am to tell you. Meet our friend at Napoleon's House in New Orleans at 1 P.M. on Tuesday. Do you understand?"

"Yes, I do. Thank you, Maria. We will talk soon."

Sean hung up and considered the request to meet in New Orleans. He had expected Miami or even Houston, but New Orleans seemed too convenient. It might be that even a boss like Lou Cicero needed backing with another boss like Augie Valenti, so go to the town of the biggest boss around, Giovanni Pesce.

When Bubba came to get Sean, he got into the truck and said, "Janey and I are leaving for New Orleans this afternoon."

On the way out of town, Bubba stopped by a park on the Mississippi River outside Plaquemine. Sean threw the next to the last burner phone in the water.

Bubba told Sean on the drive back to the cabin that a lawyer from Tampa, Florida appeared at the police station for the cartel guy. According to his cousin, Benjy, the guy refused to even provide his name. Bubba also said that another Mac-10 automatic had been found in the Escalade. Sean related that the Feds would be sending agents down.

Bubba and Sean continued driving in silence for a while. Finally, Bubba said, "You can't go to New Orleans alone. I need to back you up one more time."

Chapter Fifteen
Resolution

Bubba and Sean arrived back at the cabin by late morning. Janey was awake and moving so the three sat down to discuss their plans. Sean started the conversation.

"I need to go to New Orleans to meet with Lou Cicero and, hopefully, John Valenti. At this point, it is unclear who will be there. I am to meet him tomorrow at Napoleon's House Bar in the French Quarter. I am curious as to why Cicero chose New Orleans. It is like he knew we were nearby. It might also be that Valenti would feel comfortable in Pesce's town. Both Pesce and Cicero were friends of Valenti's father."

Bubba interjected, "I never really asked about this, but you are meeting Lou Cicero, the mob boss from Miami? And you think that Pesce, the boss of New Orleans, is in on the meeting?"

"I can't be sure that Pesce is involved, or if he is offering protection. Both Pesce and Cicero were at Gus Valenti's funeral, and John Valenti had warm relations with both of them."

"Anyway, we need to get a hotel room in New Orleans for at least two nights. Of course, we have no internet and we need to avoid using our names, until we know things are safe."

"Don't worry about getting rooms. I will get two rooms under my name at the Royal Orleans. The manager is an old friend. It is at the corner of St. Louis and Royal streets in the French Quarter. It is also very close to Napoleon's House."

"Bubba, I can't ask that of you. You have done enough."

"I want to see my niece taken care of." Bubba smiled at Janey. "Although she might think about staying here."

"No way are you going to leave me out of the trip to New Orleans. The immediate danger is gone. A change of residence seems logical."

"Agreed. Let me make a couple calls."

Bubba then stepped outside the cabin with his cell phone.

Janey looked at Sean. "Do you feel safe going into the den of mobsters?"

"I really don't think I have a choice. There is a target on my back and the only way to remove it is from someone with leverage against Augie Valenti, and that is Lou Cicero, another boss.

"I do not believe that Valenti would try anything in Pesce's backyard or while I am under the protections of Cicero. It is the logical decision.

"Let's get our clothes together and close up the cabin. I would like to leave in an hour or two."

Bubba came back and said that there were two rooms reserved under his name at the Royal Orleans. "I will meet you two at the hotel later. There is other business I have to attend to but let's plan on dinner together."

As Bubba was leaving, Sean walked up to Bubba and handed him two thousand dollars.

"This should cover the hotel rooms."

Bubba looked irritated. "You know that is not necessary. I am doing this to help you both. Blood relations need no money."

"Humor me please, Bubba. With all you have done, it is the least I can do to reimburse you. It is just to pay for New Orleans, and I know the Royal Orleans is not cheap."

"Please, Uncle Bubbie, take the money. It will make me feel better."

"For you, darling, I would do anything." Bubba kissed her on both cheeks and put the cash in his pocket. "See you in New Orleans."

It did not take Sean and Janey long to clean and pack up. They didn't have many clothes and the sheets and towels were one load in the washing machine.

As they were pulling away, Sean felt a little remorse at leaving their hideaway in the swamps. He hoped that one day he and Janey could stay a little longer without the oppressive feeling that they were being hunted. Sean had high hopes that this trip to New Orleans would cure that problem.

New Orleans was an hour and a half drive down the interstate highway. When they reached the exit for Canal Street, they had to crisscross through the various one-way streets of the French Quarter. Deep in the Quarter you could feel enmeshed in an 18th century city, albeit with neon lights and a parade of cars. Still, it held a magic few cities in America, or the world, could claim. Sean was looking forward to this visit with some joy, but mainly trepidation, at what the city would hold for him this time.

The Royal Orleans had the classic French Quarter hotel look

with white washed stucco and black wrought iron balconies. The doorman in front was dressed in the dark hotel uniform, and they left the car with him to valet. Sean knew that the cost to park the car was as much as a cheap room in town.

When they reached the front desk, Janey told them the name of Bubba LaPlante, and the assistant manager showed up to take them to their room. On the way, he made conversation with Janey. When he discovered she was Bubba's niece, his Cajun lilt started, and Sean discovered that Janey could put on the same accent. In Houston, she never used it, but being back in the bayous brought out the Cajun girl. Sean liked it and he thought it made Janey even sexier.

Their room was a small suite with a balcony. It was luxurious and comfortable. Sean tipped the manager twenty dollars and he continued smiling at Janey, obviously smitten with her Cajun charms. No sooner was the door closed, then Janey started shedding her clothes. Sean was up to the prospect of an afternoon delight, but Janey had other ideas.

"I am going to go soak in the big tub with some bubble bath. That small shower at the cabin did not cut it. Come and get me in an hour or so."

"Well then, I guess I will head out on the streets of the Quarter. I will pick up some wine while I am out."

Sean loved walking in the Quarter. There's always something going on, and there was a bar or restaurant around every corner. Finding a wine store could be difficult, but the concierge at the hotel pointed him in the right direction.

When Sean returned to the room. Janey had finished her bath. He showed her two bottles of Pinot Noir he had picked up.

Janey said, "Does the offer of an afternoon delight still stand?"

"Let me jump in the shower. Why don't you open one of the Pinots and I'll meet you in bed."

Sean finished his shower, sipped some Pinot and started kissing Janey from her full firm breasts down her flat stomach to her neatly trimmed blonde triangle. He used his tongue until Janey came. Sean then pulled her to the edge of the bed and inserted himself into her. This continued until both were spent. They then laid on the bed enjoying the late afternoon light through the shades.

While they were propped up, drinking their wine, Janey turned to Sean.

"What do you think is going to happen tomorrow? Better yet, what do you hope will happen tomorrow?"

"My best hope is that Cicero has reached out to John's Uncle Augie and has the outline of a settlement. John is going to have to back off his separate plans for Houston. Uncle Augie is going to have to take a step back as well. Maybe John can go work with Cicero in Miami or Pesce in New Orleans.

"As for me, I just want Augie to recognize that I was not setting up this crime family with John in Houston. That is where Lou Cicero will be most important."

There was a knock on the door. Sean threw some shorts on and before he could open the door, Bubba identified himself. As Sean opened the door, Bubba said, "Y'all get dressed up in the best duds you brought. Meet me in the lobby in an hour."

Sean and Janey scraped together the best clothes available. Sean had a pair of beige cargo pants, tropical shirt, and a lightweight jacket. Janey wore a sundress and a light sweater.

Bubba showed up in dressier wear: slacks, a sportscoat and exotic skin cowboy boots. Bubba explained the skin was from a nutria, the large water rodent that now infested the bayous. The skin was black, hairy, tough, and waterproof.

Bubba suggested they go to Muriel's, a place known for its ghosts as well as its Cajun food. It was a short walk from the Royal Orleans to Muriel's location on the corner of Jackson Square. The walk provided some visuals of the varied local entertainers—musicians, jugglers, dancers, and artists. Since Halloween was only a few days away, there were stranger costumes than usual. Sean loved the show that New Orleans could provide. Now he thought about the difficult day ahead, and it made his shoulder hurt.

When the three of them were seated and cocktails were ordered, Bubba took control of the conversation.

"Tomorrow you need to be aware that you will be transported for your meeting somewhere. As you are well aware, no organized crime boss is going to do anything in a public place, particularly Pesce or Cicero.

"I will try to stay back and watch what happens at Napoleon's House. I do not want to risk either you or me going crosswise with these guys. Since you have one burner phone left, you should take it. They may take it away, but you can note that no one knows the number. Do not use it prior to leaving. Tell Cicero that you need to stay in touch with Janey and her uncle who provided your safety and support."

"That is the truth. I do not fear going with Cicero. Maybe I am a fool, but I do not believe he would allow me to be hurt."

"Maybe so, but there are other actors involved who many not have the warm and fuzzies for a lawyer tied to a renegade mafia soldier."

Sean thought this last statement by Bubba a little strange since he did not remember talking about John Valenti going rogue. Curious, but it might have been something Janey said to him.

After the drinks were served, Bubba raised his glass.

"Here is to a successful conclusion to your troubles. Let's not dwell on it anymore and enjoy the meal."

Muriel's food did not disappoint. Sean's entrée of Crawfish Étouffée was spicy and delicious. Everyone at the table was happy and content by meal's end.

After the meal, Bubba suggested that they go to an upstairs room for an after-dinner drink. The room they entered was dark and had Egyptian and Voodoo relics. Bubba explained that it was a room where seances took place, and that ghosts were welcome. Bubba encouraged Sean to go seek advice from the fortune teller at a table. She wore a gypsy outfit with a head scarf and had piercing eyes. A deck of Tarot cards was in front of the teller and she asked Sean to cut the deck. He did as requested and she started turning the cards.

"You have been in grave danger. There is a way out of your troubles, but all may not be as it seems. Trust the one you have known the best."

Sean was taken aback at the specifics of this reading. He paid twenty dollars and returned to the table with Bubba and Janey. Sean told them that the fortune teller told him his troubles were going to end. He was not going to frame this encounter as anything more than a carnival act.

After drinks, the three of them walked around Jackson Square, then headed for the hotel. Sean knew he needed rest to be sharp in the morning.

Sean and Janey took the morning slow. They met Bubba at ten in the lobby and headed to Café du Monde, which was famous for its Chicory coffee and beignets. While sipping coffee and brushing powdered sugar from the beignets off their clothes, they talked about the day. Bubba said he would be on surveillance for Sean, but out of sight to avoid issues. It was agreed that Janey would stay at the hotel. Sean was going to go early for a table.

When they returned to the hotel, Janey had a tearful goodbye for Sean. He took the last burner phone but did not turn it on. He also wrote Bubba's phone number and the hotel phone number on a piece of paper to put in his wallet. Sean told Janey, "Don't worry. I feel good about this. I will let you know something by tonight or I may see you."

He kissed her deeply and hugged her, then left the hotel.

It was a short walk to Napoleon's House. It was an old brick house reputed to have been set up as Napoleon's residence in exile in the early 1800s. Napoleon never made it, but the bar and restaurant maintained the historical claim.

Sean was a half hour early. He requested a table outside in the courtyard and sipped on a Dixie beer. Right on time, Lou Cicero appeared and worked his way over to Sean's table. An obvious bodyguard stayed by the doorway. Cicero sat down and requested a Sazerac Manhattan from the waiter.

"This is a real mess you have stepped in Sean. I know that

you did not intend to be part of John's plans. Word on the street put you there though.

"I have worked to get you absolved of blame. However, you need to be part of the resolution with John. This means you are going with me to meet with John.

"Let's not speak any more about this until we are moving. Enjoy your beer and tell me about your adventure since being shot. By the way, how is your shoulder?"

"It still hurts but the bullet passed through with minimal damage. How did you know?"

Cicero smiled. "You know I have ways to find out what I need to know. I find the fact that you were targeted particularly upsetting."

The waiter brought Cicero's drink and Sean gave an overview of his escape from Houston, hiding in the swamps and setting a trap for the cartel hitmen. Sean mentioned that the Feds would be picking up the surviving shooter.

Cicero remarked, "I do not believe that he will do well in federal custody. He violated a cardinal rule for would-be hit men. Do not get caught."

Sean and Cicero talked about New Orleans, the weather and anything other than what Sean wanted to talk about—the plan to get resolution. Just before Cicero finished his drink, he signaled to the guy at the door to get the vehicle.

Sean paid the tab and then walked out to the street. There was another black Cadillac Escalade. Sean and Cicero got into the rear seats. The rear seats were captain's chairs, which provided great comfort and support. *At least we are traveling in style,* thought Sean.

As the driver was negotiating his way out of the French Quarter, Sean finally asked, "Where are we going?"

"We are driving to a place called Venice. It is located near the mouth of the Mississippi delta, famous for its inshore and offshore fishing.

"However, that is not our agenda. Pesce owns a house there. They call it 'Fish House' because of his nickname. It is isolated. He is able to control any prying eyes and ears. He also has a secure internet there tied to a private satellite. Pretty sweet actually."

"Is Pesce going to be part of our meeting? Is John coming in?"

"Hold on. I will explain. First, Pesce will not be joining us. He has arranged everything though.

"John needs to be called. He wants to hear from you when you were with me. He will be provided instructions on finding the house. As for as I know, John is in New Orleans.

"It was felt by all concerned that it was too risky to have John and Augie together at the same place. That is why Augie will be on a telecom connection.

"As you know, the grievances on both sides may be difficult to resolve. Augie complains that John tried to set up a new family, he was controlling the drugs going through Texas, and the two brothers were seeking to end Augie's time as boss of the Kansas City family.

"John has legitimate grievances as well. Augie killed his brother, and tried to kill him, and you. It appears that Augie has been forcing John out of the family business for a while.

"I have an idea how to proceed and I will act as a mediator.

Now, let's get John on the phone."

Cicero told the passenger in front to provide the phone in the glove box. "This is a burner phone. I have a number to a phone that John is using." As Cicero called the number, Sean remembered his burner phone, but decided that need to be kept secret for the time being. Cicero put the small flip phone to his ear.

"Hello, John. Good to talk with you. We are on our way to the Fish house. Yes, he is right here."

Cicero held the phone out to Sean, who put it up to his ear. "John?"

"Counselor, you okay? It is good to talk with you. Things got a little dirty. Sorry about that. I wanted to be sure that you would be going to this 'sit down.' Hopefully, Lou can work something out because I am out of options. Put Lou back on."

Sean handed the phone back to Cicero.

"Okay, John. I am handing the phone to one of my men who will provide the coordinates. See you there."

Cicero handed the phone back to the passenger in front and told him to provide the latitude and longitude coordinates.

Cicero looked at Sean. "Once he plugs the coordinates into Google Maps, he will find the place, along with directions."

Sean observed that their route was leaving the New Orleans suburbs and headed down the flat delta. There were fields of rice, corn, and sorghum. Sean recounted his geography studies and remembered that the Mississippi delta pushed out quite far into the Gulf of Mexico. The Mississippi is a big river and moves a lot of dirt. Sean also remembered that this area was periodically scraped clean by hurricanes.

They continued on the highway going southeast. The number of farms and houses started diminishing. As the highway went close to the water, there were marinas with shrimp and fishing boats. After a couple of hours, the highway seemed to end into a collection of houses built on stilts surrounding an active marina with obvious sportfishing boats. There were shallow draft boats used for bay fishing of redfish and speckled trout. There were also some forty-foot-plus boats used for offshore fishing of tuna, swordfish, wahoo, kingfish, and the occasional marlin. Sean was fond of offshore fishing.

Too bad I have the business to take care of thought Sean.

In the farthest point of the marina, just before it flowed into open waters, stood one house separate from the rest. It had a large car park in front and a boathouse in the rear. It appeared larger than most of the other houses and appeared to have more activity. There were a few SUVs, trucks, and black sedans out front with some big men standing around. Cicero told his driver to pull up front next to steep stairs leading to the front door. The guards obviously knew Cicero and approached Sean. Cicero spoke to the guards.

"That's my lawyer. He has permission from Pesce to be here."

The guards asked about cell phones. Sean told them he had a burner phone and they put it in a lead box by the base of the stairs. They said he could get it later.

Cicero commented, "I am surprised you brought a cell phone."

"Only because I might need to call the lady who came with me to New Orleans."

Cicero just grunted and they went up the stairs and into the house. There was an arching vaulted ceiling in the entry way which led into a large room with windows on two sides looking out at the water. Sitting on an expansive sectional couch was one man, sharply dressed in all black.

When Cicero approached, he stood, and they kissed each other on either cheek, a formal Italian greeting.

"This is Vito Pesce, son of Giovanni Pesce, in whose beautiful home we are meeting."

Sean extended his hand and Vito shook it vigorously.

"Nice to meet you. You have had an interesting time getting here, or so I have been told."

Vito smiled. He was a dark handsome man, in the Italian movie star style. The black clothes only added to the overall impression.

Sean replied, "It has been a strange ride, that is for sure."

Cicero remarked, "He is carrying a war wound as well. A bullet passed through his shoulder. An inch either way and he might have been history."

"Let us see if we can't prevent that from ever happening again. Can I offer you a drink?"

Vito went up to the well-stocked bar and poured Johnnie Walker Black all around with ice. The three men took their drinks and sat down on the couch.

Sean noticed a huge blue fin tuna mounted on the wall across from the windows. "Nice fish. Do you do much offshore fishing here?"

"That is one of the main reasons for the house out here at the ends of the earth. There is a forty-foot Viking fishing boat in the boat house."

"Nice boat. I could spend all of my time and money on bill fishing and die a happy man."

"You and my father seem to have a similar mind set. He is down here whenever the fish are running." Vito looked at Cicero. "You have gone with my father a few times."

Cicero nodded. "Beautiful boat and it affords lots of privacy."

The light was changing outside, and dusk was settling in. An orange and purple cast was spreading across the sky.

There was the sound of the front door opening and John Valenti entered the room. Both Cicero and Vito greeted John with a kiss on either cheek. Sean approached John and shook his hand.

"What, no kiss?"

"I am not that kind of lawyer."

Everyone laughed. Vito got John a drink and they all sat down together. Cicero took control of the conversation.

"I am glad you decided to come, John. There is no positive to this war with your Uncle Augie."

"Speaking of Uncle Augie, is he coming here?"

"No. That would not have been the smart move. You might have made a move against him or he might have done the same. Pesce did not want blood spilled on his turf."

"How are we to resolve our differences?"

"There is a room above the boathouse here that has a secure satellite communication connection. Your uncle is standing by to get on a video conference.

"Before we go there, I need to know what you have figured out in terms of a solution."

John shifted nervously, then started speaking slowly. "I will separate myself from the KC family. My intent was to set up in Houston and work with the San Miguel Cartel. I would work with all the families—Miami, New Orleans, New York, whoever."

Cicero leaned in toward John. "You know that Houston is to remain an open city so that we all can take advantage of its assets. This was the ruling of the Council." John looked at Cicero, pleading his case. "Lou, you are a member. Why can't I act as a liaison there? There is more than enough to share with all. It is also growing fast and will offer more advantage to come.

"Sean, help me here. Don't you think that the other Families could use Houston, if I just kept to my corner?"

Sean looked at Lou Cicero, Vito Pesce, and then John Valenti. "I do not have a dog in this hunt. This a matter outside my area. My expertise is representing people after mistakes have been made. I do not know how restrictions are set on Family activities. This is your playing field, and your associates, and I am only here to get myself out of harm's way."

Vito now interjected. "John, you have a narrow view of the restriction placed on the Families to stay out of Houston. Sure, you could carve a niche for yourself and say you won't go farther, but that is not what our history has shown us. Once a family gets established, anyone else has to pay a tribute. This is a matter that needs to be addressed by the Council of Families."

It was obvious that this conversation was making Valenti nervous. Cicero decided to placate Valenti.

"I will approach the tribunal on your behalf. First, let's get things ironed out with Augie. It is almost six and time for our call."

Cicero stood up. Sean and John stood as well. Vito stayed in the room, noting they did not need his input.

Cicero, John, and Sean crossed the deck in the back and went down the stairs to the boathouse. Daylight was quickly fading, and the back of the house was quite dark.

When they reached the boathouse, Cicero opened the door and told John and Sean to come in. "I am just looking for the light switch."

Sean entered the boathouse and could make out the looming presence of the big fishing boat. His eyes were just adjusting to the darkness when he saw a shadow move to his left. He heard a muffled sound, like a strong whisper, and John Valenti fell to the ground in front of Sean. This happened so suddenly that Sean could not help stumbling over John's body.

Sean was on the ground next to John's body. He was so stunned that he did not immediately react. He did get a chance to briefly see the outline of the man in the shadows before he exited.

Suddenly the lights came on in the boathouse and Cicero walked up to Sean. John was laying on his stomach, his eyes were open, and a slow trickle of blood was coming from a hole behind his right ear.

Sean yelled at Cicero. "Can we help him! Is he dead?"

Cicero offered a hand to Sean to get up. When Sean was on his feet, Cicero put an arm over Sean's shoulder.

"There was nothing to be done. John had to go. This goes beyond Augie. This was the will of the Council."

Cicero helped Sean to the stairs that went to a room in the top of the boathouse.

"Come with me and I will explain."

Chapter Sixteen
After the Storm

Cicero had to hold Sean's elbow as he climbed the stairs. Sean was dazed. He didn't think he was hurt. He just felt like his brain was scrambled.

The room they entered had no window but had a leather couch and chairs facing a big television screen. There was host of electronics below the screen.

"Why didn't we try to reach Augie Valenti to prevent this?"

Cicero was at the bar in the corner pouring a couple glasses of scotch.

"It would have done no good. John Valenti thought he could do as he wanted. The problem with Augie was secondary to ignoring the dictates of the Council.

"Every organization has to have rules to govern its members and maintain its structure. What separates our Families from the cartels are those rules. The organizations would slide into anarchy if we did not have rules of function and enforcement of those rules. The rules that govern our organization are like the structures that maintain chain of command in the army.

"There is a reason that the original Mafia families copied

the Roman legions. You have commanders who are the bosses of the Family. The capos are the officers who see that orders are carried out, and the soldiers do the work on the ground.

"John Valenti was a capo who wanted to be a boss. If he had left that within the Kansas City Family, things might have ended differently.

"John would not heed the warnings he was given. I personally reached out to him. He insisted on setting up a Houston organization. Now, many of the Families have representatives that work through Houston but there is no controlling group or Family.

"Despite repeated warnings from the Council and me, John insisted on being involved with that fentanyl. That is wrong on many levels. It kills the customers you are trying to reach with the products. It also draws too much attention from the Feds.

"Finally, John was integrating that goddamn San Miguel Cartel as partners in his Houston business. You can buy product from these cartels, but do not become partners."

Cicero hesitated and took a long drink of his scotch. "There was a personal reason as well. When John had Carla clipped, it was unnecessary. She was tougher than most of the men and would have never snitched. I counseled against any action, but John did not listen. Carla was a friend for many years."

Cicero ceased talking and seemed momentarily to be emotional, something Sean had not seen before. Cicero snapped out of it quickly.

"When this shooting happened in Houston, the Council decided that John had to go. Augie missed his chance. I am sorry that you had to be in the middle of it, but you now have a free pass from Augie and the Council."

Sean sat dumbfounded at this justification for the assassination of John Valenti. He heard the "free pass" but wondered what the Council might do now that he was privy to one of its executions.

Almost as if he sensed Sean's fears, Cicero addressed the issue.

"You are in no personal danger from the Council since you were an unwilling participant. Augie made a hasty judgment call against you, with no facts. For this bad decision, the Council levied a one-hundred-thousand-dollar tax on Augie to be paid to you."

Sean was shocked. He was like the guy released from Death Row who gets money for his time there. Sean had to ask what was at the forefront in his mind.

"What is the Council? I have an idea but I would like you to explain."

"It is composed of bosses of several Families, who set the rules we will all follow to do business. It is what has kept the Mafia business afloat and minimizing conflict between Families."

"And you are a member?"

"Yes. There is no group meeting like what the old Dons did in the past. Now we get encrypted messages regarding a problem and reply in a like manner. If discussions are necessary, we use secure technology." Cicero pointed at the huge television screen and the associated computer equipment in the room with them.

"There is a danger of government hacking, but we hire the best geeks available. There is no schedule and the meetings are often held on less than twenty-four-hours' notice. Cicero had been on the edge of the leather chair during most of his speech. He now settled back in the chair and sipped on his scotch.

"Let's talk about you, Sean. You now know many things that can cause you to be a liability. I am vouching for your continued silence."

Sean looked at Cicero. "I understand completely. It will be one more attorney-client confidence I take to my grave. I just hope it is not soon."

Cicero smiled. "Like I said, you have nothing to fear now. You will remain my lawyer. You will also handle any issues in Houston that other Family members encounter."

"What happened down there? John fell like a statue, but there was no blood I could see."

Cicero sat forward in his chair.

"I will answer only because you were in the middle of things. Valenti was shot behind the ear by a pro with a high velocity small caliber gun. There was a silencer, of course. The bullet goes into the skull and instantly kills the person. There is very little blood loss."

"What happens to his body and what about his bodyguards?"

Cicero sighed. "Do not worry about that. Vito is going fishing offshore in the morning, and John will be a guest. As for the Valenti bodyguards, they have accepted positions back with Kansas City. Good enough?

"There are some things you will be responsible to do. First, I am sure you were going to do this anyway, but you need to go to the cops and the Feds. They will want to know about the shooting at your office. Tell them you have been hiding out for your safety and have received an all clear from a client with knowledge. Keep it in the attorney-client privilege.

"Second, I would advise you to leave on an extended vacation after you debrief with the Feds. Take that pretty girlfriend and go visit Italy or France. We are requesting this because we want to see everything cool off. 'Out of sight, out of mind.'

" Finally, I know you are going to be inclined to limit or get out of the criminal defense business, but that would not be a good choice for a while. The Council will feel better if you maintain the status quo. Remember to tell yourself, 'This is the life I have chosen.'"

Sean was shocked to hear that his professional life was now subject to rules and restrictions set by the Council of Mafia bosses. He would have to closely weigh all options, but he needed to signify assent now.

"I understand. As far as what has transpired, I was never here."

Sean picked up his glass and realized that that he had drained it.

"I will take another scotch if you are pouring."

Cicero got up from his chair and picked up Sean's glass. He went to the bar and poured two more glasses of scotch. Both Cicero and Sean downed the whiskey quietly.

Cicero put the glasses on the bar.

"Time for us to exit. You can call your girlfriend from the road."

When Sean came down the stairs, the lights were on and there was activity. One of Pesce's guards was cleaning the tiles with a bleach solution that Sean could readily detect by the smell. There was no sign of John Valenti's body.

Vito was on the big cabin cruiser and he lifted a hand to wave at Sean. Sean returned the wave and observed Vito was getting the boat ready to go out. Sean followed Cicero out of the door of the boat house and walked toward the main house.

Sean had been in the boathouse for less than an hour. Sean knew that his life would never be the same, but he could tell no one. This was his cross to bear.

Sean retrieved his phone at the front door. The driver pulled the Escalade up front and there was the same passenger in the front seat. After Cicero and Sean were in the vehicle, the passenger told Cicero, "The Valenti guards are no longer a problem." Sean knew not to ask any questions and Cicero just nodded his head, then spoke to Sean.

"Wait until we are out of the Venice area to call your sweetie." Now it was time for Sean to nod his head.

When they were in the delta farmlands, Cicero gave the thumbs-up for Sean to call. He called the room phone at the Royal Orleans.

"Sean? It is so good to hear your voice. Are you okay?"

"Everything is fine. I should be back at the hotel in a couple of hours. We will talk then."

"Okay. See you then."

Sean hung up. Cicero put his hand out.

"Please give me the phone."

Cicero took the phone apart. He handed the pieces to the passenger, who threw all of it out the window into some water by the road.

"As we discussed Sean, no one knows shit about the Fish house. Let's keep it that way."

"Understand."

The drive back into New Orleans was silent. Sean was busy with his own thoughts and Cicero reverted to his usual quiet persona. In fact, Sean had never seen Cicero talk as much as he had in the past day. It was comforting to Sean for Cicero to return to his quiet self.

As they were pulling up to the Royal Orleans, Cicero turned to Sean.

"You are strong. This has been a lot to handle, but you will be fine. Contact Mr. Green if anything appears out of line with the government when you meet with them."

Cicero reached out and patted Sean on the cheek, then he shook his hand.

"Be well, Sean."

"You too, Lou."

Sean got out of the Escalade when the doorman opened the door. The Escalade continued out the hotel drive. Sean went through the lobby and up to the room. He knocked rather than use the key and Janey answered immediately. She threw her arms around his neck and gave him a wet kiss on the lips.

Sean came in and sat in on the bed.

"Before I debrief to you, let's get a couple of glasses of wine and sit on the balcony."

When they were situated outside, Sean started his narrative.

"Cicero took me to a house far out on the Mississippi delta. This prevented any possible eavesdropping by the government.

"Valenti showed up and we all had a discussion. My concern

was to get the target off my back. Lou Cicero arranged for my safety and it was agreed to by Augie Valenti, who is Johns' uncle, and the cause of our problems.

"Once my fears were alleviated, I let the others deal with Valenti. I did not want to be part of any negotiations with John. When I left, John Valenti was still there." Sean said this knowing it was true, maybe not alive, but still at the Fish house.

"Oh, there is some frosting on this cake. For wrongfully targeting me, I am to receive a one hundred-thousand-dollar benefit."

Janey looked surprised.

"All I care about is that you are safe. The money is well-earned."

Janey raised her glass to toast and Sean reciprocated.

"Before we get involved in any celebration, I need to go talk with your uncle. I will be back shortly."

Sean walked down the hall to Bubba's room and knocked on the door. Bubba answered with a grin and bear hug for Sean.

"I am glad to see you. You look no worse for the journey."

"May I come in, Bubba? There is something I would like to discuss with you."

Bubba opened the door and Sean entered Bubba's suite.

"Come in and sit down. Let me get you a drink."

Sean took a seat on the couch while Bubba went to the bar in the room and poured a couple of scotches with ice. He set the glass on the table in front of Sean and then sat in the big arm chair next to the couch.

"Okay. What's up?"

"I went through a traumatic episode at the residence where

I was taken. I have sworn to keep everything confidential, but with you, I probably do not need to worry because you know what happened."

Bubba's face darkened and he meekly protested. "I don't know what you are talking about. No one told me anything."

Sean put down the drink and looked right at Bubba, then his nutria-skin boots.

"It was the boots that gave you away. The problem with one-of-a-kind boots is that it is like a fingerprint. I thought I recognized your truck when we first got to the Fish house, but there are lots of Dodge Ram trucks around.

"When Valenti was shot, I tripped over him in the dark. That put my face near the floor and I caught sight of the shooter's boots as he headed towards the light." Sean pointed at Bubba's boots. "And those are the boots I saw."

Bubba sat quiet and stone-faced. Neither of them said anything for a while.

"I could deny it, but you are too smart for that. There was nothing personal. It was just a job.

"I have done freelance work for the Pesce family for many years. They contacted me for this job and then I realized who it was. Neither Pesce nor Cicero wanted a Family member to do this shooting.

"When I realized your connection, it made me more certain to take the job to keep you safe. I did not know how far the Family might take this vendetta and hoped I could be helpful if you became a target.

"Once Cicero and the Fish realized my connection to you, they were in agreement with my role. Cicero likes you. He made sure you were separated from John Valenti and what he was accused of doing.

"Anyway, if it had not been me, it would have been someone else. John Valenti was a marked man."

"How long have you been in on this, Bubba?"

"I received word on the contract the same day I set the trap for the cartel shooters. In fact, since I speak some Spanish, that is why I went to the jail while you made your calls from Plaquemine. My role was to tell him to shut up and bail would be arranged. That is never going to happen. There is now a contract on the cartel kid. He will not last long at the federal lock-up in Houston."

"Does Janey know your role with the Pesce Family?"

"Of course not, and I would appreciate you not saying anything about it."

"You have my word, Bubba. Since I am disavowing everything that occurred at the Fish house, I might as well forget you ever had a role."

"Thanks."

Sean stood up and shook Bubba's hand.

"Words cannot express the gratitude I have for all you have done. I hope we can continue as friends."

"Take good care of Janey and you will always be welcome in the bayous." Sean walked toward the door and then turned to Bubba. "Is there anything else I need to worry about with you?"

Bubba laughed. "No. I am just a good ol' Cajun with underworld contacts. Not so unusual here."

Bubba patted Sean on the shoulder. "Go make that pretty girl happy."

Sean walked down the hall and entered the room.

Janey was dressed in one of her naughty outfits she wore in the club; push-up bra and thong panties. Sean smiled and embraced her.

"Before we get too involved in fooling around, I would like to talk with you. Please put on a T-shirt and sit with me on the couch."

Janey felt a little disappointed but did as she was asked. Sean went and poured the last of the wine into their glasses.

"When we return to Houston in the morning, I have to go meet with the federal and state authorities. They will grill me for information on the shootings. I do not intend to hide any facts surrounding the shooting or our escape to Louisiana. You will have to be named as my nurse, and savior.

"They may talk to you, but relay only what we did, not what we discussed. There really is nothing to fear. We even helped arrest one of the killers for them.

"I will go back to my law practice, but I am going to give it a couple weeks to tie down cases that can be resolved. All the other cases will be delayed until after the beginning of the year, such as my case in Laredo.

"I need a break. How would you like to go to Europe for six weeks?"

Janey jumped on Sean and kissed him deeply on the lips.

"Does that answer your question?"

"Good. Now that I have a financial cushion, I will pay your rent for the next couple months. You find someone to care for your place.

"One of my first priorities will be to get my travel agent working on the details."

Sean now reached for Janey's hand and led her to the bed to celebrate the end of this traumatic chapter in their relationship and lives. Sean thought, *Where one chapter ends, a new one begins. This one starts with hope, travel, and discovery.* Sean smiled at Janey and allowed himself to get into the pleasure of the moment.

Acknowledgments

This novel would not have been possible without the contributions of Diana Barron, who took my handwritten legal pads and turned them into a completed manuscript, and Darla Coons, who provided emotional support and some good editing.